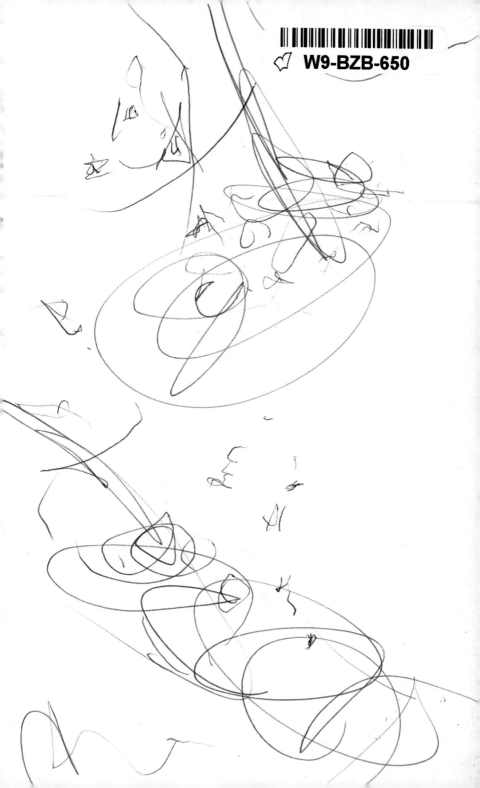

W9-BZB-650

Truth
with a
Capital
T

Truth
with a
Capital
T

Bethany Hegedus

DELACORTE PRESS

Visit us on the Web! www.randomhouse.com/kids
Educators and librarians, for a variety of teaching tools,
visit us at www.randomhouse.com/teachers

Library of Congress Cataloging-in-Publication Data
Hegedus, Bethany.
Truth with a capital T / Bethany Hegedus. — 1st ed.
p. cm.
Summary: Staying with her grandparents over the summer while her parents are on tour for their latest book, eleven-year-old Maebelle struggles to find her true talent and tries to compete with her newly adopted African American cousin.
ISBN 978-0-385-73837-8 (hc : alk. paper) —
ISBN 978-0-375-89409-1 (e-book) —
ISBN 978-0-385-90725-5 (glb : alk. paper) [1. Individuality—Fiction. 2. Adoption—Fiction. 3. Cousins—Fiction. 4. Grandparents—Fiction. 5. African Americans—Fiction.] I. Title.
PZ7.H35894Tr 2010   [Fic]—dc22   2009040043

The text of this book is set in 12¼-point Adobe Caslon.
Book design by Vikki Sheatsley
Printed in the United States of America
10 9 8 7 6 5 4 3 2 1

First Edition

For DawnMarie,
a dear friend and honky-tonk angel

And for Norma Fox Mazer,
who believed early on

· 1 ·

Little-Known Fact:
A hippo can hold its breath for a
really long time.

I wish Mama and Daddy could.

I pressed my forehead to the bus window. It left a smudge, but I didn't care. I was riding a Peach—a Georgia Peach. All the buses in the fleet had gigantic peaches painted on the sides. The bus was decked out. There were four flat-screen TVs bolted to the ceiling and scattered throughout the bus. Of all things, a repeat of *Good Afternoon, Atlanta* featuring an interview with Mama and Daddy had come on ten minutes ago.

Mama and Daddy had made arrangements for me to sit in the front seat behind the driver where she could keep an eye on me. But as we waited for the last passenger to reboard the bus at our fourth Waffle House stop, I stood.

I went to slip Grace, the wrinkly bus driver, a five, a move I had seen Daddy do at fancy restaurants to get a good table—but he used Ben Franklins. As in hundred-dollar bills!

Grace laughed a deep Coca-Cola chuckle as she shooed the money away.

"Thanks, Maebelle, but no thanks. I can't be bought, but I can be persuaded." Grace kept on, "I tell you what, we've got another girl traveling solo. Take a seat near her, next to the toilet," she said, though her pronunciation of *toilet* sounded like *twa-let*.

I nodded. Getting away from the sound of Mama and Daddy's TV voices would be super-great.

"All righty now, go ahead. But don't forget, *these* eyes"—Grace pointed to her eyes, which were hidden behind big sunglasses—"can see you anywhere."

"Yes ma'am, thank you ma'am," I said.

I grabbed my backpack with my name, Maebelle T. Earl, embroidered crookedly (yes, it was my handiwork) on the zipper pouch and carted it down the long bus aisle, then took a seat diagonal and one back from the girl Grace had mentioned. She was asleep—dead asleep. She had one of those travel pillows wrapped around her neck and a bag of snack mix in her lap. Her hand was still inside it and a bit of drool was creeping out the side of her mouth. *G-r-o-s-s,* gross. Had she fallen asleep midbite?

I plopped down as Grace revved the engine and took off for another lonely stretch of highway. I scootched around in my seat and did my best to settle in. At least back here, I figured I wouldn't be able to hear Mama and Daddy spout their self-help talk.

I was wrong.

"The third step in our Making Our Love Last series is to face one another, breathe deeply, and to try to match the intake and outtake of your breath with your partner's," Mama's voice said from the nearest TV as I dug in my book bag.

I reckoned there was nowhere to run. Mama and Daddy's fame was spreading. They had just left for a nationwide book tour that kicked off in New York City, and they were being interviewed on the *Today* show and *Regis and Kelly.* The publisher was so happy, they'd sent a limo to the house to take Mama and Daddy to the airport. I rode in it too, before they dropped me at the bus station. I may have had a *T* in my name, like everyone on Mama's talented side of the family does, but in my case, my middle initial stood for NO TALENT. As in not a lick.

Not anymore.

This fall, when I started school at Robert E. Lee Middle, I was going to be in *regular* classes. Regular! No more Gifted and Talented program for me. I'd been kicked out. Or as Mama had explained it when we went over the official letter that arrived two days before, I was "not pegged this year."

That night, we'd had a family meeting, Daddy in his wingback chair with Mama perched on the arm and me on the couch.

"Darling, tell us how you feel," Mama'd said.

"Fine," I said. They didn't believe me.

They told me it was A-OK if I didn't want to talk

about it. That in time I would. And that maybe a summer away would even do me good. In the meantime, they let me know I was more than fine the way I was and that as long as I did my best, my best was good enough.

I didn't swallow a word of it. My best made me regular, not gifted or talented. I was normal, as in nothing special. Truth be told, that was what had my chin hanging so low. Not traveling via bus or being without Mama and Daddy for the summer.

"Tweedle, Georgia," I whispered to myself. That was where this bus was headed, or at least where I was: Tweedle, Georgia.

I couldn't wait to see Granny and Gramps. Mama and Daddy were therapists and they said all the right things, but that was because they had to. They were trained to. When I needed cheering, I often talked to my grandparents. Even over their crackly cell phone, they were the two biggest cheerleaders any girl could have.

I stopped digging in my backpack and hauled out what I was hunting for: my hardcover copy of *Little-Known Facts on Just About Everything* and the spiral notebook I carried with me where I jotted down my favorite fact finds. I uncapped my lucky purple pen and was all set to get to studying, but it was hard to focus on the bumpy bus. The words bounced around the page as Mama's voice droned from the TV, "Inhale. Exhale. Breathe new breath into your marriage. Feel the love."

Feel the love! Blech.

"Why, would you just look at them?" The girl diagonal from me had awoken when that last semi passed us. "I wonder what it's like to be in love." She crunched, eating while she talked. She offered me some of her snack mix.

I shook my head. "Maybe it's just an act for TV," I said. "Did you ever think of that?"

Mama and Daddy did love each other, and the work they did was good; it was important. It kept families together. I just wasn't in the mood to hear one of their fans—and a young one, at that—gush over them.

"Naw, that's real love. I can tell," said the girl, a crumb stuck to her lower lip. She wiped it away with the back of her hand. "You ever been in love?"

"Nope." The only thing I'd ever loved was test taking, but by the time I turned eleven my scores had slipped from hundreds to nineties to eighty-fives, which wasn't good enough for G & T. I reckoned I was in trouble long before the middle-school placement test came my way.

"One day I want to fall in love," the snack-mix girl said. "And when I do I want it to stick. Forever. For keeps! Just like them."

The girl pointed at the screen, where Mama and Daddy continued their breathing exercises. "Want to breathe with me?" she asked.

Was she nuts? I *was* breathing.

I ignored her and got back to reading, burying my head in my book. Ranjeet Malone, my best friend, was still in G & T. I hadn't told her yet that I wouldn't be. It was too embarrassing for words. I flipped the pages, memorizing anything and everything that caught my eye: *A blue whale's heart is as big as a small car. Flies take off backward.* And *A hippopotamus can hold its breath for five minutes.* I jotted that one down and repeated those facts over and over and over.

I could feel myself getting smarter. I could. And maybe if I got smart enough, maybe when the summer was over I could take that placement test again. Maybe.

· 2 ·

Little-Known Fact:
Sideburns, the hair that some
men grow on their cheeks, are
named after Union general
Andrew Burnside.

I prefer Gramps's beard.

The bus turned off Highway 181 and I saw the sign:

TWEEDLE, GEORGIA

FOUNDED IN 1835

BIRTHPLACE OF CHARLES TURNER, CONFEDERATE GENERAL

We turned onto Greene Street and then onto Main. There were a ton of what Daddy would call mom-and-pop stores—Frank's Eggs and Grits, Betty's Bait and Tackle, Claire's Crispy Fried Fritters, and Turner's Restored Turntables and All Other Appliances, just to name a few. They dotted each side of the street. *Quaint* was what Mama would've called it.

I was more than happy to be staying the entire summer

in a place like this. I had even told Gramps and Granny that when they'd invited me over the phone.

"I can't wait to come. On one condition," I'd said.

"What's that?" Gramps asked.

"That I have you all to myself."

"*Ha!*" Gramps chuckled. "You don't have to worry about that! Who else would have us?" he'd asked.

When I hung up, Mama'd reassured me that Isaac, my newly adopted ten-year-old cousin, was staying with Aunt Alice in Chicago. "He's had enough upheaval in the last year," Mama said, "so Alice wants him with her."

So it was just me. Good!

I scootched onto my knees, balancing on the bus seat, hoping to catch sight of Winnie, Granny and Gramps's Winnebago.

"Maebelle, sit your booty down," Grace hollered from the front of the bus.

She wasn't kidding. She did have eyes in the back of her head.

"This isn't a gymnasium, you know."

"Yes, ma'am."

I did as Grace instructed, but I kept my eyes peeled. I expected to see Winnie parked along the curb somewhere on the way, standing majestic, like the glorious hunk of metal she was. But nope, I didn't see her.

A throng of folks filled the depot parking lot. Up front a lady with a toddler slung on her hip waved an American flag. This had to be a hero's welcome.

I hadn't spotted any soldiers when I'd moved to the back of the bus, but now I saw him. He was sitting four or five seats in front of me on the same side. He had been dozing with a hat over his head when I had walked by.

The crowd parted as Grace pulled the bus into the lot and came to a complete stop. A whoosh sounded as she opened the front doors.

"Those passengers departing in Tweedle, Georgia, grab your gear. We're here," she announced. "Girls, that means the both of you."

Several people spilled into the aisle. The buzz-cut soldier and some lady in a denim dress, and the love-struck girl in front of me. I tapped my foot as I hiked my backpack over my shoulder. If I had stayed up front, I would've been off the bus and wrapped tightly in one of Gramps's big bear hugs by now. No matter how tall I got, he always managed to get me up and off the ground.

The love-struck snack-mix girl was struggling to get her duffel bag down from the overhead area. I tried to scoot around her, half squeezing into an empty seat, but my backpack smacked her one.

"Ouch. Where's the fire?" the girl said. She had on the oddest outfit, a pink pair of coveralls like the kind mechanics wore over their clothes.

"Sorry, Ruth," I said, using the name sewn on her chest pocket. "I thought you could use some help."

For a minute she looked ready to fight, like some girls I had seen on the playground at recess, but then her face changed.

The grin on her face made her look excited, not angry. "How'd you know my name? Are you psychic? I've never met a real psychic before. I've seen them on talk shows, though. I love talk shows. I watch them with my mom. She kind of got me hooked on them. They give all sorts of good advice. So is that what you are—a kid psychic?"

Kid psychic? Was she kidding?

"Um, it's written right there." I pointed. "On your pocket."

"Oh, yeah, right. I forgot about that." She glanced at her chest, reading her name, and walked slowly down the aisle. "This is new. My first time wearing it. It's a gift. So what's your name?" she asked, acting like we had all day.

"Maebelle T." I didn't stick out my hand.

"Nice to meet you, Maebelle T. You know, even though you read my name, you could still be psychic. You have that look about you. Deep and kind of sad."

"I'm not sad," I said, puffing out my chest. "Not in the least bit."

"So you don't know why I'm here?"

I scrunched my brows together like crinkle-cut French fries. "Here? On the bus?" Ugh, I had to hurry. What could I say to get this girl out of my way? "Let me see. You're here on a visit, right? To see a loved one?"

"See, you are a psychic!" she said in a voice of pure amazement. "How'd you know? How does it work? Can you teach me?"

Simple. I had made a good guess—she was here for the same reason I was: a summer visit. But I didn't tell her that. Instead, I bowed my head like I was the most mysterious swami ever to ride a Georgia Peach bus.

"That's for me to know and you to find out," I said.

· 3 ·

Little-Known Facts:
The name Crayola is a combination of two French words meaning "oily" and "chalk."
Amiga is the Spanish word for *friend*.

I need friends more than I need crayons.

I was the last one off the bus, but I hopped the three stairs anyway. I almost ended up in heap on the ground, but I did a little hop-skip move and somehow remained fully upright. I expected to hear Gramps holler, "There she is! Maebelle! My one and only!"—his special nickname for me—above Granny's clapping and the sound of her truck-driver whistle as Gramps spun me around, but nope. When I took my first two steps in Tweedle there was no applause. No ruckus.

Unless you counted Ruth.

"Cool save," she said as she trailed at my heels and asked me if I did gymnastics and if so where did I take tumbling, because she loved tumbling and wasn't it funny that we had that in common but that it shouldn't come as any surprise to me since I was an all-knowing swami, after all.

Shoot. Even Ruth had a talent. She could talk the ear off an alligator.

"I don't take tumbling." I showed her my *Little-Known Facts* book. "I've got better things to do. I'm studying for a big test—well, if I can retake it."

"But it's summer," Ruth said.

I thought she might ask me more, like what kind of test, but she didn't. She chewed her bottom lip and kicked her foot, heel to toe.

"I take tumbling and thought practicing round-offs and stuff might be the kind of thing friends do . . . I mean, if you want to be my friend. . . . We know a lot about each other. You're a psychic who likes to read and study and I'm a boy-crazy cartwheeler who likes snack mix and talk shows."

She raised her brows, hopeful.

"Yeah, sure, we can be friends." What was I supposed to say—no? I hadn't made a friend so quickly since Gina Sullivan shared her sand shovel with me back in kindergarten. I shrugged. "I don't know anyone else in town."

"Me either," said Ruth. "I came over my spring break, but the kids in Tweedle were still in school. I thought when I was out everyone was, but I guess it's a state-by-state thing." Ruth prattled on, and I only half listened as

I searched the crowd for Gramps and Granny. "I live in Chattanooga, Tennessee."

I grabbed my suitcase and tried to fight my way through the crowd. The soldier grabbed his khaki bag and raised it high in the air. He let out a loud "HOOO-RAH! I'm home!" The crowd went wild, crying and clapping and waving mini–American flags pasted on Popsicle sticks. The soldier stuck his cap on his toddler daughter's head and looped his wife in for a hug.

"Listen," I yelled over the band to Ruth, who was still talking, "I've got to find my grandparents."

The crowd pressed in, all knees and elbows and overgrown instruments like tubas and trombones. I dodged them as best I could and climbed up on a bench near the depot doors. No sign of Granny or Gramps. I didn't even spot Winnie, and you couldn't miss that Winnebago. She was as old as the hills and backfired something fierce. But Gramps wouldn't give up driving her, even now that the Rootin' Tootin' Bootin' Band was no more.

"Miss Winnie hasn't conked out yet. Besides, she is part of the family," he would say whenever Mama nagged him to trade Winnie in for a newer model.

I stood on the bench and searched the crowd. Ruth had found her dad, who was busy talking with Grace, the bus driver. Grace held out a clipboard and I saw Ruth's daddy write on the papers. I didn't have anyone to sign for me! Where were Granny and Gramps?

The marching band began to play "God Bless the USA" while the hometown hero finished his hugging and high-fiving. He gathered his wife and toddler and helped them into their 4×4 truck. Then he popped behind the wheel and laid on the horn, giving it three short blasts as folks on the sidelines took pictures or videos. He cranked the truck and drove away. Soon the marching band and the crowd took off too, but the Georgia Peach was still parked in the gravel lot, refueling and allowing new passengers to board.

Streamers and confetti littered the ground. With the crowd thinning I expected to see Gramps decked out in his favorite shorts and sandals and Granny in a prairie skirt, her gray hair all flyaway in the wind, elbowing those who had been blocking them from me.

Nope. No "Outta my way!" commotion.

I hopped to the ground and took a seat on the bench. Ruth dropped her dad's hand and ran over to me. She stopped before she skidded into the bench. She had to be hot in that getup of hers. "Maybe we can sign for you."

"No need to sign. Really, I'm fine." I yanked some change out of my zippered pouch. I planned to call Granny and Gramps if they didn't show up s-o-o-n, soon. Grace had a schedule to keep. "You go with your daddy."

"How'd you know he was my dad?" Ruth's eyes grew as round as yo-yos.

"I guess he could've been your uncle or an older third cousin or something but"—I held my palm up to my forehead like I'd seen Johnny Carson, this old-time TV host Gramps loved watching on TV Land at my house in Atlanta, do when he did Carnac the Magnificent sketch—"my third eye told me otherwise."

"Anyway, my grandparents will be here soon. That guy

washing the windows told me they called and would be here any minute," I fibbed.

My shoulders drooped. This wasn't how my arrival was supposed to go. For the first time, Ruth eyed me like I wasn't telling the whole truth and nothing but.

"How soon?"

"He didn't know." I bucked up, making my voice as chipper as I could. "But my psychic powers tell me ten minutes, is all."

"Okay! But you call me if you need me," she said. "The number is 706 . . ."

"555–1130," I finished. The number was on the outside of her phone. And the phone had been propped up on her leg, facing me as we chatted on the bus.

Ruth stood there gobsmacked, as if she had just discovered pigs really could fly and she was watching one do it.

"Maebelle, even before I met you, my mom told me that this summer, something BIG was going to happen. You are a part of that BIG thing. I just know it!" She took off running backward and then shouted, "Meet me tomorrow afternoon at three o'clock at the swimming hole. Maybe we'll run into some boys!"

I nodded, but who knew. I had no idea where the swimming hole was, and I surely didn't care about meeting any boys. Besides, if Granny and Gramps didn't show I could still be here at the depot, twiddling my thumbs in downtown Tweedle.

· 4 ·

Little-Known Fact:
The actor Nicolas Cage ate a live
cockroach in one of his movies.

Ick! Gross. I like to eat Snickers.

G race couldn't hold the bus any longer. She called the
Georgia Peach headquarters, and when they couldn't
reach Gramps and Granny, the employee who worked at
the Tweedle ticket counter had to sign for me. It was *m-o-
r-t-i-f-y-i-n-g*, mortifying. Thank heavens, Ruth had already headed home. She would've discovered that my
psychic abilities stunk.

If I'd really been a mind reader, I would have known
where Granny and Gramps were. I'd been sitting on this
stupid depot bench for a good twenty minutes. I'd called
their house from the pay phone. It just rang and rang.
Finally, their voice mail clicked on.

"Yoo-howdy. It's me? Where are you?"

The second message I left on the cell Mama had
insisted they get.

"Hello! It's me. The one and only Maebelle T. Where are you? Did Winnie get a flat or something? I'm at the depot. I don't know where you live or I'd walk there. Is it close? Are y'all coming? You didn't forget about me, did you?"

I hung up, feeling worse than I had before I called.

I sat back on the bench. In forty-five minutes I drank a total of three Coca-Colas and ate two Snickers from the vending machine. The ticket guy inside the depot kept eyeing me, but so far so good, he didn't come poking my way. Ask me, it had something to do with the way I kept my arms crossed and the leave-me-alone look I had perfected backstage at Mama and Daddy's weekend retreats. I didn't mind being *their* errand girl, but I wasn't going to fetch stuff for anyone else. The couples who volunteered at their Breathing and Being Boot Camps thought they could order me around, ask me to make copies or fetch more name tags from the hotel cart.

Nope. I did two things and two things only. One: I kept Mama and Daddy's podium stocked with bottled waters and Kleenex, so they could replenish themselves and hand tissues to the crying couples they dragged onstage with them. And two: I was the sound-check girl. I got to test the audience microphones before the retreat started.

"Paterson, party of two," I'd say, like I was a hostess at the Olive Garden or somewhere. The rest of the time I splashed in the pool or did crossword puzzles online.

I wished I had a microphone right now. "Eberlee, party of two! Granny and Gramps!" The Used-to-Be-Best Grandparents Ever! "Where are you?"

Yep, I'd said it aloud. Screamed it, rather. The ticket guy heard me. "Everything okay out here?" he asked, stepping out the open depot door.

"Nope—I mean *yes,* yes, sir," I said, forgetting my manners. I sounded like Chicago-born Isaac, who never said sir!

He squinted, like he was trying to place me. I guessed in as small a town as this, the ticket fella knew everyone who came and went. "Name's Giles," he said.

"Maebelle," I said. "Maebelle T. Earl."

"I'm sure your grandparents will be here soon." He plunked his hands on his hips and stared into the distance. "They sound just like my wife. Ever since getting pregnant she's losing track of time. We're having our first. If he comes early, I don't know what Amelia will do!"

Giles the chatterbox had it all wrong. Granny and Gramps were professionals. Lots of musicians showed up willy-nilly, but Gramps said they got most of their bookings because even though they weren't tied to a clock, they knew others were. Being on time was a sign of respect.

"Yeah, well, they never had to pick me up before. They always come to our house. Mama doesn't like Winnie getting parked in our drive, but there isn't much she can do about it."

"Winnie? As in Winnebago? Are you talking about the Rootin' Tootin' Band retirees? The ones who took up residence in old Edith Eberlee's house?"

"Yes, sir."

"Why didn't you say so! Everyone around town knows

who they are! Old Edith was a recluse, so it was a shock to hear she had relatives who once sang at the Opry. Your grandparents are practically legends. The town is abuzz with their arrival, but everyone has been too shy to give them a warm howdy and hello."

"Don't be," I said. "They're happy to put down roots after years of traveling. Plus, they're the nicest two folks you will ever meet."

"Well, they left Tweedle early this morning. They filled up"—he pointed to the one gas station in town, opposite the one stoplight—"and I ain't seen or heard their Winnebago since."

I gulped down a burp. The Snickers I'd eaten and the Coca-Colas I'd guzzled were making return appearances, like Granny and Gramps when they went out onstage for an encore.

"Could they have had an accident?" I asked. "Is that why we haven't heard from them?"

Giles took me by the shoulders and sat me down. "I'm going to be a terrible father—look at me, scaring the dickens out of you! Listen, you hear that?" He tipped his head toward the inside of the depot where some country radio station was playing. "That's been on all day. There haven't been any accidents. They would have announced it. So you get those thoughts outta your head. I'm sure there is some reasonable explanation as to why they ain't here yet."

"Maybe."

"Of course there is. Things don't always go according to plan."

"Ain't that the truth," I said, thinking about Ranjeet darting off to the G & T hallway without me.

"See. So there must be some holdup, but not to worry, I am sure your grand*padres* are on their way."

"Yeah, I reckon."

The sun disappeared behind a cluster of clouds, and I started to hear a rumble way off in the distance.

Boom-bam! Bam-boom! Boom-boom-boom-bam!

My ears pricked up. Nope, that wasn't thunder. That sound was one sound and one sound only: Winnie!

The knots that were pretzeled up in my stomach slowly untied.

Gramps pulled down Main and honked Winnie's horn. It was rigged to play the chorus of their most famous song, "Hoedown Showdown."

Go on ahead and kick up those heels!
Cut yourself loose and see how it feels!
Pick your team right 'cause it's Saturday night—
Welcome to the hoedown showdown!

"See, there they are," said Giles, above the recording. "I've danced to that song on the jukebox many a time."

I cocked my arm and got to waving. A hand waved fast and furious back at me. It wasn't Granny's or Gramps's. It was a hand I hadn't expected to see for another six months, not until Christmastime rolled back around.

Granny pulled Winnie to a stop right in front of the depot. "So sorry we're late, Creamed Corn," she said through the open window. A second later Isaac bounded out of the Winnebago, leaving both Giles and me speechless.

"Yeah, it's all my fault," Isaac said. "My plane got delayed—bad weather—but I'm here now. Surprise, cuz!"

· 5 ·

Little-Known Fact:
Houseflies hum in the key of F.

That is the sum total of my musical knowledge.

Surprise? I was surprised, all right. So much so that I dropped my *Little-Known Facts on Just About Everything*. There was at least one fact I didn't know: what was Isaac doing here? No one had said anything about his coming to Tweedle. Not Granny or Gramps. Not Mama or Daddy. And I had asked—outright.

Isaac hugged me around the middle. I was only a year older than he was, but I was tall for my age and Isaac was a bona fide peanut. He barely came up to my armpits.

"Hey there," I said, dumbstruck. Finally, he dropped his arms.

Granny hopped out of Winnie next, and instead of doing her truck-driver whistle while Gramps spun me around, she went straight over to Giles and shook his hand.

"Thank you for keeping an eye on our Butter Bean

here." She ruffled my hair and gave me a side hug. "We were stuck at the airport, picking up our grandson, and our blasted cell phone ran out of juice."

Giles's eyes got wide looking at Isaac and then at Granny. I had a feeling it wasn't because Isaac was short and the rest of us were redwood-tree tall but because Isaac's skin color didn't match ours.

We hadn't gotten that look in Chicago, but we had been there so short a time, just for Christmas Eve and Christmas Day, that the only places we'd gone were to church and for a drive along Michigan Avenue to see the fancy lights and the holiday windows at Marshall Field's. If Granny noticed the questioning in Giles's eyes, she didn't comment on it. She went right on talking, reciting Isaac's long list of accomplishments by way of introduction, including his being a great trumpet player and ending with one that was news to me: "He just played at Symphony Center in Chicago—to a standing ovation."

A standing ovation at Symphony Center—holy cannoli.

Isaac wasn't even really related to Granny and Gramps. How had he gotten the talented gene?

"Well, ain't that something," said Giles, his face easing into a genuine smile. "I love the trumpet. I'm a fan of all music. Jazz. Country. Classical. I am what the wife calls a connoisseur." Giles turned to me. "Are you musical too, Maebelle?"

"Oh, Maebelle here has many talents, but music isn't one of them." Granny chucked my chin. She meant it lovingly, but still, it did nothing but embarrass me.

"Listen, I hate to cut this short," I said, giving Giles a

mighty fast handshake, "but can you go grab that paper-work so Granny can sign for me? Then we've got to get going. Gramps has got to be hot sitting in Winnie."

"Oh, he's napping. He conked out a while ago," Isaac said.

"Yeah, well, I can't wait to see great old, old Aunt Edith's house. And Cotton, I've missed that dog a ton," I said, not wanting to wait a second longer to smother Granny and Gramps's dog with kisses and cuddles.

Granny signed some slip of paper on a clipboard and showed Giles her ID—so he could be sure she was who she said she was, even though after she showed up in Winnie there was no mistaking she was a member of the Rootin' Tootin' Bootin' Band. After some more small talk on famous musicians—and Giles going on and on about how he hoped his baby boy would play the guitar or wail like Waylon Jennings—I grabbed my suitcase and Granny's hand, leaving Isaac right where he was. In the parking lot.

If only we could have left him there for good.

But nope. Isaac ran after us. "Maebelle, your book. Don't forget your book."

I snatched my *Little-Known Facts* book from him and stuck it under my arm.

"Thanks" was all I said.

· 6 ·

Little-Known Fact:
The Library of Congress has
wings named after Thomas
Jefferson, John Adams, and
James Madison.

Do only presidents get wings
named after them?

Old Aunt Edith's place was practically a mansion. There was the wraparound porch and four Cracker Barrel–looking rocking chairs, two on each side of the front door. There were a ton of plants, shrubs, and hanging baskets. Everything about the place was bigger and grander than I thought it would be.

Not only was it big, it was the only house on Azalea Avenue where the driveway still wasn't paved. Both sides were lined with six mighty oak trees. It looked like something out of a book—*The Secret Garden* or *Gone with the Wind,* or a new book nobody had written yet that was a combination of them both. Those pictures Granny had e-mailed to Mama didn't do it justice.

"Here we are. Last stop, Casa de Eberlee," Gramps said, sounding not groggy at all after waking from his snooze.

We piled out of Winnie. Gramps ushered us in the front door and we dropped our belongings in the hallway—or foyer, since it was fancy-schmancy and had a crystal chandelier hanging from the ceiling. "The kitchen is straight through the parlor, and the patio and the rest of the backyard is thataway." Gramps pointed up the stairs. "Up there, we've got the bedrooms, and above that we've got an attic that a long time ago was turned into a nursery."

"For plants?" I asked.

"Nope. A nursery for kids. Some of my kinfolk must've had twins or cousins close in age, like the two of you, because there were double baby bassinets and baptismal gowns and other stuff tucked up there. There isn't a pool, but I hear there is a swimming hole not too far from here for when you want to take a dip."

"Didn't you spend summers here when you were a kid?" I asked. Mama and Granny had gone through some of the particulars of the family relations, but I just didn't get it.

"There's a snapshot of me about age four in the music room, but I don't ever recall coming here," Gramps said. "The music room and the drawing room are through that door over in the east wing."

"Wings? The White House has wings! This is too cool. This place is huge." Isaac glanced around, taking in the open rooms and the long staircase and the grandfather clock that stood in the entryway. He turned and pointed to a wooden door with an old-timey brass lock. "What's back there in the west wing? President Obama? You get it, Maebelle—West Wing?" Isaac elbowed me.

"I got it." I grimaced.

"Nope, no presidents, modern-day or otherwise. Just more knickknacks and antiques. Old-lady stuff, I'm sure," Gramps said.

"What? You haven't been back there?" I asked, edging in for a closer look.

Gramps stepped in front of the door. Granny stood beside him. Mama and Daddy taught that technique in their marriage classes. It was called Presenting a United Front.

"It was Edith's wish to leave that wing closed off," Granny said. Her eyes darted from Gramps to the door and back, as if something downright suspicious was going on.

"Hey, Isaac." I elbowed him. "Maybe this place is haunted. Maybe crazy old Edith was a serial killer and she stashed dead bodies back there."

Isaac backed into Granny, as if what I'd said could totally have been true. She settled him, resting her hands on his shoulders. "Don't be silly, Turnip Toes."

"Then why did she order that wing kept closed?" Isaac's eyes got wide, like he had seen a flying saucer, or a man with a chain saw running through the center of town.

"Oh, Edith probably closed it off when central heating and air-conditioning were added—years ago," Gramps explained. "It must cost a pretty penny to cool and heat this place."

"And though I am not too superstitious," Granny said, "I believe it is best to honor the wishes of our dearly departed kin."

"Lest they come back to haunt us." Gramps growled from the back of his throat to do his best to scare us.

Isaac laughed at Gramps's gentle teasing, and I did too. Before we'd headed inside, Gramps had quickly given me one of his special bone-crushing hugs. I wished he had spun me around, but I guessed he'd been too eager to get us in the house.

"Where's Cotton?" I asked, looking around for Granny and Gramps's big old basset hound. "Aunt Edith's will didn't say no dogs allowed, did it?"

Gramps sat on one of the entryway stairs and tugged on his beard. "Oh, we had another change of plans. Isaac here is allergic to dogs, so Cotton is staying in Casa de Backyard, outside."

"What?" I stuck my *Little-Known Facts* book under my arm. I liked to carry it with me wherever I went. I turned to Isaac. "That dog is family!"

"Cotton doesn't need to sleep outside. I can take a pill," Isaac offered. "Alice sent me with some."

"Good. You do that," I said. "Cotton can't sleep outside!"

"Maebelle Tanya—"

"Earl," Gramps said, joining Granny. They had used my full name. Uh-oh.

The crinkles around Gramps's eyes went hard and then soft. He pulled me onto his lap and brushed my bangs out of my eyes. "That pooch has been by my side over ten years now, but Isaac is allergic and it's his first time here—"

"It's my first time too."

"It's his first time *staying with us*." Gramps raised one of his fluffy eyebrows. He was one hairy man. "We don't want anything to ruin it, do we?"

I bit my lip.

Granny laid her hand on my shoulder. I was trapped.

"No, we wouldn't want that," I said. I reckoned no one cared if my trip wasn't going gangbusters as long as Isaac was happy.

"That's my girl," Gramps said. He tweaked my nose, nipping at its tip. When I was way little and he did the same move, I'd run to Mama and cry into her lap, thinking he'd really stolen my nose. Even though I hadn't cried into Mama's skirt in years, a part of me wanted to. Gramps had called me "my girl," not "my one and only."

I stared at the floor and caught sight of my toenails, which I'd painted pink special for my arrival. "May I go out back and say hey to Cotton? I don't want him to think I forgot about him."

"Of course, Sugar Snap, go ahead." Granny picked up my backpack and hoisted it over her shoulder. "We'll get you unpacked and show Isaac to his room. Dinner is in half an hour, so don't get too dirty. I fried up a mess of chicken this morning. I figured we could have a picnic at the kitchen table tonight."

"Yum," I said. I loved Granny's fried chicken and Gramps's potato salad, but after those Snickers, I wasn't sure I could muster up much of an appetite.

"Do you like fried chicken, Isaac?" Granny asked.

"I sure do," Isaac said. "And since it's a picnic tonight, I'll make deviled eggs. My mom taught me how."

"Perfectamundo." Gramps thumped him on the back. "That will be a sensational addition to the welcome party we have planned."

I didn't stay to watch the three of them head upstairs together. I barreled outside and found Cotton curled up in the shade of a clump of pine trees. He was old and his hearing wasn't so good, so my footfall didn't wake him. When I plopped down next to him, my butt must have rattled the ground. He blinked his eyes, inched over, and licked my leg.

"Glad to see you too, boy," I said, nuzzling the top of his head. "Plenty glad."

· 7 ·

Little-Known Fact:
The country singer Patsy Cline
lived in nineteen different towns
before she was fifteen.

I've only ever lived in one place—
Atlanta. Isaac, too—Chicago. That's
one thing we have in common.

That night, Granny tucked me in. I'd never slept over with Granny and Gramps before; there was room in Winnie, but Mama thought it improper for me to sleep in such a "contraption." "No child of mine is going to sleep in a rolling tin can. You can drive around in her, but sleeping, no."

Granny smoothed back my bangs. "Butter Bean, are you ever going to forgive your gramps and me for being late?"

"I called the house," I said. "And your cell."

"I know," Granny said. "I heard your messages when

you and Isaac were unpacking. I'm so sorry we weren't there to welcome you. You must've been scared."

"I wasn't scared for myself—just worried about y'all. I had no idea where you were or if you even remembered I was coming."

"How could we forget? We have been so looking forward to your visit."

I scrunched myself up and leaned against the headboard. Mama would like the room I was staying in. It was covered in chintz and had lace doilies. It was proper in all respects.

I was glad Gramps and Granny were staying put, but this place, as big and as grand as it was, didn't feel like theirs. It needed some curtains made of silver sequins or some denim couch cushions.

"Gramps and I feel just awful. Isaac too. What a way to welcome you to town." Granny smoothed my bangs again—the same way Mama did when they got too long. "At least that Giles fellow was friendly. Was he good company?"

"Not as good as Cotton. I feel bad that he's sleeping outside. What if it rains?"

"He's on the screened-in porch. That pooch is just fine."

"But what if he gets lonely?"

I tucked my fingers in my armpits and glared at the closed bathroom door. Isaac's room adjoined mine. Through the bathroom! A bathroom we had to share! Gramps said it was called a suite in the old days, but to me there was nothing "sweet" about it. I'd have rather we slept on opposite ends of the house. If that locked wing hadn't been off limits, I would have asked for a room down there.

"I suppose if the weather gets too bad we can put Cotton in the laundry room. I don't love him being outside either, but Isaac's been through enough. We don't need to aggravate his allergies on top of everything else."

"I still don't understand why no one told me . . ." I mouthed the next words: *that he was coming.*

"There simply wasn't time. Alice only called us the day before last." Granny kept her voice quiet. "And we expect you to get with the program, Turnip Toes—be warm and welcoming."

"Fine." I grimaced. Granny had a ton of nicknames for me, but Turnip Toes was my least favorite. "But couldn't he have come to visit later? After Mama and Daddy were done with their book tour?"

"Just like your mama and daddy *had* to go on that there book tour now, Alice *had* to talk at that symposium in Switzerland when their main speaker canceled. She couldn't turn it down, and Isaac asked to come here—to spend some time with you, with us."

"But there are ski slopes and hot chocolate in Switzerland. I'd want to go there."

I wouldn't have wanted to. Not really. Not unless Granny and Gramps were going too.

"Yeah, well, Summer Squash, it wouldn't all be hot chocolate and snowflakes for Isaac. Going to a cancer symposium after he lost his mother to breast cancer doesn't sound like much fun for a ten-year-old boy, now, does it?"

I shrugged. "No."

Granny ran her hands along the thin cotton bedspread that covered my legs. "Sure, Alice was their neighbor and their friend, she pitched in when Isaac's mother was sick, but that isn't the same thing as her being his sole caretaker. Isaac's had a lot to adjust to, and in such a short period of time."

"I guess." I got quiet, listening to Isaac brush his teeth.

It hadn't really struck me that he'd never see his mother again. Ever. That *my* family was *his* family. That we were all he had.

"So do your gramps and me a favor." Granny tapped the bed. "Make Isaac feel at home here."

"How? I'm not even at home here." I picked up the doily on the nightstand. "This place is *s-t-u-f-f-y*, stuffy. It's like a museum."

Granny raised her brows. Mama did the same thing when I gave her lip.

"Yes, ma'am," I said. "I'll make him feel at home here."

"Good. Gramps and I knew we could count on you." She kissed my cheek and then went and rapped her knuckles on the bathroom door. "Are you about finished up in there?" she asked Isaac through the closed door. "It's getting late. Bedtime."

"Ah-huh," Isaac said over the running water. He must have still been brushing his teeth. When he finished, the ancient faucet stopped its banging.

It got quiet for a minute, but then Isaac opened the door to my room. He stuck his head in. "Can we sleep with the bathroom doors cracked?"

"Sure," said Granny, before I could get out a big fat no. "Maebelle won't mind."

She followed Isaac into his room. I'd seen it earlier. It was decked out just like mine. All lacy and old-lady-y. Ick.

Granny must have sat on his bed just like she did mine. They talked quietly to one another, but even with the doors cracked, I couldn't quite hear.

I thought about getting out of bed and spying, to see if Isaac got a goodnight kiss too, but the wrought-iron bed I was sleeping in would squeak and give me away. So I thumbed through my *Little-Known Facts* book, looking for something to jot down in my notebook with my lucky purple pen. I found some interesting information, stuff that might cheer Isaac up. Just then Granny closed the outer hallway door to Isaac's room and then she stopped by mine.

"Lights out," she said, flicking the switch near the door.

"Yes, ma'am." I curled up under the covers, glad this old house had air-conditioning, and kept my finger on the page that I'd been reading.

When I was sure she was back downstairs, probably sharing a cup of tea with Gramps, I whispered loudly, "Isaac, you up?"

"Yeah," he answered. I could barely hear him, but he sounded kind of sad. Was he missing his mama? Aunt Alice? Or both? I missed my parents. Isaac and I had both gotten phone calls after dinner, but I'd see my mama again. Isaac would never see his.

"Good. I want to read you something." I flipped on my

bedside lamp, grabbed my book, and flipped through a few pages. "There were many famous orphans throughout history. Leo Tolstoy, the famous Russian writer of *War and Peace,* the world's longest novel, for one, and Johann Sebastian Bach, the Baroque musician and composer, for another. Cool, huh?"

Isaac must've gotten out of bed to hear me better. He leaned against the doorjamb and that old, old, old night-light of Aunt Edith's cast a yellowish glow around him.

"Why are you telling me that?" he asked, so quiet I barely heard him.

"I just started memorizing little-known facts. You've got to work the brain, like any muscle."

"That's cool," he said. "But just so you know, even though my mom is dead, my dad's not." I reckoned he no longer needed the bathroom doors left open to sleep in a strange bed in the middle of nowhere, because he added, "So I'm not an orphan, and that's a fact." And with that he shut the door.

· 8 ·

Little-Known Fact:
In 1861, the Confederate Post Office (the South refused to use the U.S. Post Office!) introduced Rebel stamps. They cost five cents.

If I could get my hands on one, I'd sell it for a ton!

Early the next morning, I let Cotton out from the screened-in porch so he could run around and do his morning business.

"Go ahead, boy," I said.

Cotton bounded onto the patio and then leapt off of the small wooden incline so he could putter away in the lush grass. It was so green it looked like a golf course. Cotton disappeared behind a shrub—I reckoned he was private and didn't want me to see him do a doggie number-two—so I pushed through the fence gate, propping it open. I explored the side yard, knowing Cotton would follow me when he was good and ready.

Over here there were lilac bushes, green pointy-leafed shrubs, and a cascade of ivy that clung to a latticework trellis that rested against the side of the house. I tried to peek in a window that looked like it was at the end of the locked wing. The drapes were heavy fabric—maybe even velvet—and I couldn't see a thing.

I was going to get in there whether old Aunt Edith wanted me to or not. *Little-Known Fact: Casanova, the lady killer (as in making the women swoon, not killing them, like Jack the Ripper) was a spy in Italy in the 1700s!* I bet in his time he learned to get into a locked castle or two.

Cotton barked and ran ahead of me. I followed.

The dewy grass was wet beneath my bare feet. It tickled my toes. I liked this part of the morning—early, before anyone got up. It felt new and clean. Like a test paper before the teacher ordered you to write your name on it.

I circled around to the front of the house and went to grab the morning paper, the *Tweedle Gazette*, from the drive. I nabbed it and then stared up at the house. The veranda had four columns—Southern architects used them a lot, copying the ones used by Greeks in the ancient old days. (That was something I'd learned in G & T.)

The two-story house came to a point at the way top, leaving room above the second floor for a high, slope-ceilinged attic. A white ironwork fence ran the length of the balcony, and there were even a few twisty iron pieces lining the bottom porch. A fancy black wrought-iron chandelier hung above the heavy wooden front door, which was framed by two smaller columns.

I leaned against one of the trees that guarded the drive and slapped my thighs. "Cotton, c'mere, boy."

He came waddling from the back, going as fast as his short, stubby basset hound legs would let him go. He stopped at my ankles, and I crouched and pointed his snout toward the front stairs so he could get a good look at the house.

"Look at those columns, Cotton. I was right when I thought this place reminded me of Tara from *Gone with the Wind*. I bet anything this house is antebellum. How cool is that?"

"What's antebellum?" asked a voice above me.

I about leapt right out of my skin. *Heavens!* But it was just Isaac up there in that tree. I hadn't even seen him, nestled between the tree branches, spying on me.

"You trying to scare the devil outta me?" I said, using one of Mama's expressions that she must've got from Granny, because Mama never talked clipped like that. She always spoke in full syllables, sounding each one out, as if she was on TV or in front of an audience.

"Sorry. I've been up here a little while. Everyone was still asleep, so I came out here to practice." He held up his horn and it glinted in the morning sunlight.

"You planning on rousing the whole neighborhood?"

"I wasn't playing! I've just been practicing my fingering," Isaac said. He tucked his trumpet under his arm and climbed down to a lower branch where he could easily leap to the ground. He squatted as he landed and popped to standing, quicker than a jack-in-the-box. "So what were you saying to that dog?"

"'That dog' has a name, and it's Cotton." I hugged Cotton, who'd been sitting quietly at my feet. "He got named that 'cause he's so friendly he takes a cotton to darn near everyone."

I remembered what Granny said about me being nice to Isaac, to make him feel at home here. I'd failed last night, but I could try it again.

"Go ahead, boy, give him a lick."

"*Boo-roo-roo,*" Cotton howled.

Isaac backed away as Cotton lunged forward.

I'd forgotten that Isaac was allergic to dogs. "Ooops, sorry!" I said, pulling Cotton back an inch or so by his collar.

Poor dog—he ended up licking the air, lonesome-like. I bent down and as a treat let him lick my hand all over like it was a lollipop. I wasn't worried about germs. *Little-Known Fact: Dogs' mouths are clean, way cleaner than humans'.*

"So what were you telling him?" Isaac asked. "Cotton."

"Just that I think this house here is antebellum. That means it was built pre–Civil War."

"Pre–Civil War, huh?" Isaac looked at the house. "As in back in the slave days, you mean?"

I gulped, getting the point. Isaac was black, and the Eberlees—including old, old Edith—were white. And back in the antebellum days things were *way* different than they are now.

"Don't even think it. My father traced his family's

roots, and none of the Earls owned any slaves. Nobody has gone digging in the dirt around the Eberlee family tree, but none of the old-time Eberlees owned any slaves either," I told him, sounding surer than I felt. What was I saying? How could I be sure about a thing like that?

"Oh, really? Is that in that fact book of yours?"

"I know you're new to the family and all, but we're not like that."

"I didn't say you were *now*." Isaac danced his fingertips over his trumpet valves. "But everyone back then was. That's what the war was about—the right for people to own other people," Isaac said. "The North against the South. The North won."

I didn't need him to read the scoreboard for me. I had studied the Civil War in history.

"That they did," I said, feeling like some kind of war was going on here between Isaac and me. "But lots of folks in the South didn't believe in slavery. Some folks were fighting for states' rights."

I thought of that stamp fact I'd jotted down in my notebook. The Civil War was about slavery—everyone knew that—but wasn't it just as much about not being told what to do? Wasn't that why the Southern states seceded and made and used their own stamps?

"You wouldn't know, since you're a Yankee and all," I told Isaac, "but Southerners are big on doing their own thing."

"Yeah, Alice told me that."

Why did he call Aunt Alice by her first name, and not Granny and Gramps by theirs?

"What else did she tell you?" I asked.

Isaac kicked a pinecone that had fallen from one of the trees. He looked lost in thought. "Did you get a load of that guy at the bus station when Granny said I was her grandson?"

"Yeah, what about it?" Cotton backed up to the base of the tree and took a dump. I reckoned he'd gotten over being shy. But to give him some privacy anyway, I stepped a few feet away and motioned for Isaac to come with me.

"When Granny first introduced me, I kind of got the feeling he didn't think we could be related because you're white and I'm black," Isaac said.

So Isaac had seen it too. That weird look that had crossed Giles's face that said it was okay if Isaac was a family friend, but not if he was family.

"I bet he was just surprised, you know. No one knew you were coming," I said. *Including me!* "He was friendly and all, talking music with you." I brushed a smudge of something off Isaac's shirt. Probably dirt or dust from the tree bark. "And anyway, we're not related. Not by blood."

"But we could be related. We could be today and we could have been way back in the antebellum days or at any time in between."

For a second Isaac's eyes welled up. I didn't know what he was getting so upset over. Then he squared his shoulders and said, "It's not like stuff like that didn't happen, you know. I saw a movie about some revolutionary dude who fathered kids with one of his slaves."

"That was Thomas Jefferson." I tapped my noggin,

glad I knew who the "revolutionary dude" was. "So, honest, I don't need a history lesson."

I tugged on Cotton's collar. He was done with his business, and he trotted behind me as I stomped up the veranda stairs. Now even more than before, I wanted to snoop around the locked wing. There had to be something in there to show Isaac I knew *my* family way better than he did—or ever would!

Little-Known Fact:
Lots of folks think that the first
book written on a typewriter was
Tom Sawyer, but one historian
says it was Twain's book *Life on
the Mississippi.*

Did Mark Twain, whose real name
was Samuel Langhorne Clemens,
have a locked wing so he could
write in private?

Isaac huffed upstairs. *Let him pout,* I figured. I had better
things to do. I stayed in the foyer until he was gone and
then went straight to the locked wing's brass door handle.
I jiggled it. It wouldn't budge. The closed-off wing was
locked, all right.

I could smell a pot of coffee brewing—Granny must
have been up and in the kitchen—and I could hear
Gramps's freight-train snore rumble down the stairs. The
coast was clear.

Without anyone to bother me, I got to work. There had to be something around this museum of a house that would give me a clue to where the key to the locked wing was kept.

I checked the bookcases in the parlor first. In the movies, there were always things hidden in hollowed-out books: jewelry cases, cigars, guns. So why not a key? But nope—there was no secret stash. Not even in *The Aide-de-Camp: A Romance of the War,* which was leather-bound and looked older than dirt. I looked for a loose plank under the patterned rugs that covered the hardwood floors. There was always one of those in the movies too.

Next up was the entryway. There was a big mirror over an antique table. The table had three drawers. In the center drawer I hit the jackpot. I yanked out an old leather-bound journal that had hundreds and hundreds of pages. Inscribed on the cover in gold lettering was GUESTS OF OAK ALLEY. A gold ribbon held the place of the last names logged in. I could make out those names; they were scrawled in a handwriting that didn't look too different from the cursive we'd learned in G & T in second grade.

Jackson Millerston, guest of Edith Eberlee,
 July 4–6, 1945
Susanna Holloway, guest of Edith Eberlee,
 July 4–6, 1945
Dean Stanton, guest of Edith Eberlee,
 July 4–6, 1945
Francis Dormund, guest of Edith Eberlee,
 July 4–6, 1945

Some big party must have happened that Fourth of July. I flipped to the first entries. Throughout the log the paper was a faded yellowish brown and it crinkled almost like wax paper, but the handwriting here was fancier, full of loopedy-loops, and the ink had faded so much, the names were as dim and dull as if they had been written with a pencil.

I squinted and was able to make out a few more names.

Ambrose Mead, guest of Josiah T. Eberlee,
*   April 18–May 31, 1857*
Rose Hodges, guest of Josiah T. Eberlee,
*   January 3–Febuary 9, 1858*

And some name, Lander, who'd been a guest of Philip and Melinda Eberlee. I couldn't tell if Lander was a first or a last name or a woman or a man. I reckoned it could even have been a kid. This wasn't going to be as easy as I'd thought.

"Butter Bean," Granny called from the kitchen. "Gramps is taking you fishing. Do you want a ham and cheese biscuit to take out with you on the lake, or just a granola bar and some apples?"

I stuffed the guest book back in its deep drawer. "I'll take a biscuit, please," I called back.

Gramps had perfect timing! Going fishing was exactly what I needed—some solo time with Angus T. (for Thomas the Talented—who knew that the *T* tradition went all the way back to a guy named Josiah?) would be fine by me.

I tried not to trip on any throw rugs or bump into any bookshelves as I made my way to the kitchen. Granny stood at the counter, throwing apple- and orange-juice boxes into a cooler.

"Make yourself useful, Tater Tot," Granny said, her arms filled with food from the fridge. "Can you straighten up those newspapers for me?"

"Yes, ma'am, I sure can."

The newspaper was open to the obituaries. Glancing at the names of the recently departed—Jennifer, Rodger, Wanda—was eerie after reading the weird-sounding names from the ledger—Ambrose, Melinda, Rose, Josiah. They were all dead—had to be; 1857 was more than a century ago. More than two or three lifetimes. And to think some of those names were related to me, really related, as in once living here in this very house and having guests here for the weekend or longer. So weird!

I shuffled the newspaper sections, tapping them on the edge of the table.

"So how come we never knew Aunt Edith?" I asked.

"Hmmm . . . how can I put this?" Granny cut into a hot biscuit she had pulled from the oven. She layered some thick-cut ham and cheese between the two puffy halves. "It's like this. Some families throw their windows and screen doors wide open. Others have locked wings and barbed-wire fences."

"I haven't seen any barbed wire."

Granny got busy making another biscuit. This one she layered with Swiss cheese—Gramps's favorite. "I meant that as a metaphor, Sugar Snap."

My nose crinkled. "I don't get it."

"Just that Edith wasn't the friendly sort. No one knew

why, it's just the way she was, I guess. Your great-grandfather, Edith, and Gramps's dad, Henry T., had some kind of falling-out. Your gramps was barely in britches, so he surely hasn't been able to parcel together what the feud was about."

"Oh, I get it," I said as it dawned on me. "By 'barbed wire,' you're talking about the way Gramps's family locked stuff up and didn't talk about it."

"Exactly," Granny said. "You hit the nail on the head, Fried T'mater. I reckon your mama sure knew what she was doing when the school wanted to enroll you in G and T." Granny hugged me, giving me a brief squeeze. She kissed the top of my head. "Your gramps and I worried it would be too much pressure, but your mama wanted you to have all the chances she never got, what with us living in Winnie and driving around so much when she and Alice were kids."

The hot air that filled my belly when Granny had praised me now gave me gas. I didn't want to talk about G & T. I had made Mama promise not to tell Granny or Gramps—I'd told her I would do it while I was here, but with Isaac around I hadn't found the right time.

My stomach gurgled gas bubbles. I switched the subject back to unfriendly Edith.

"So why did old Aunt Edith leave this place to Gramps if she barely knew him?"

"You got me," Granny said. "But whatever kept Edith holed up in this place, first taking care of her aged father and then staying here herself, is beyond me. I never even heard her name until those lawyers found us playing in Halleyville, Alabama."

I plunked my elbows on the table. "Oh, I bet her lawyers hired a private detective. We should get one so we can find out facts about the folks who lived here—Aunt Edith and those way before her—back in the olden, olden days. I mean, look at this place. It's like a museum! I bet there are tons of hidden secrets to be dug up. A detective could help."

"Turnip Toes," Granny said, "don't you go getting all cinematic on me. This is not the movies, and there is no reason to track anyone down. Whatever was in the past is did, done, and over with, and that's the way your gramps wants it."

"Can't he get a locksmith or something to open the locked wing?" I got up from the table and shoved the newspapers in the blue recycling bin by the back door. I thought about Josiah T., who I hadn't known ever existed before I found the guest book. "If Gramps had a choice that didn't go against the wishes of the *d-e-a-d*, dead, I'm sure he'd make it."

"Oh, he has a choice, but he doesn't want to find out anything that's better off buried."

"What are you talking about?"

"When the lawyers read the will papers, they gave Angus a sealed envelope addressed to him from Edith."

"What do you think is in it? The key to the locked wing?"

"I don't know, Creamed Corn. It was thick like a long

letter or a lock of hair was inside, but he hasn't opened it, and I am not—*we* are not—going to push him. You got that?"

"Yes, ma'am."

"Good. Now grab me some paper napkins. Y'all can't have sticky fingers while you're fishing. I think I saw some stuffed in the back of the silverware drawer."

I shuffled through where she told me to look. The drawer was deep and messy, not organized like the entry-way table. I grabbed a stack of napkins with little red hens on them. Something was stuck to the plastic wrap. I pulled it off.

"Granny, are these yours?" I handed her the gummy stack of index-sized cards.

"Nope." She attempted to peel one of the cards from the top of the stack. It crinkled and broke apart. "What are these, anyway?"

"I don't know. I found them wedged way back there."

"Goodness," said Granny. She slid on her glasses with the pink leopard frames that hung from a black band around her neck. "I knew living in a historic home would have its share of surprises, but Brussels Sprout, you've stumbled onto a gold mine."

"That gummy stack of stuff is worth something?" I edged in for a closer look.

"Priceless is more like it." Granny separated two more cards. "They're family recipes. There is one in here for any kind of cobbler you could want: peach, blueberry, apple, and blackberry. A collard recipe, one for mutton stew, bread pudding, ham hocks, and cheese biscuits."

"Stop," Gramps said, walking into the kitchen. "You're making me hungry." He plopped the tackle box on the table. "Don't tell me you're packing all that for our little fishing expedition?"

I grabbed the recipe cards from Granny. "No, I made a discovery! Recipe cards. Do you think we should sell them on eBay or should I call *Antiques Roadshow*?"

Gramps chuckled. "You are something else, Miss Macbelle. You've got the biggest and brightest imagination. I'm not sure recipes qualify as antiques, even if they have been preserved by molasses or some such."

"Granny said they were priceless."

"And they *are* . . . not monetarily but sentimentally. That's what I meant by priceless, Celery Stalk."

Granny kissed Gramps on his bulbous nose and handed him the picnic basket. "While y'all are out on the lake, I'll steam these crusty old things." She picked one up and held it to the light. "Then I'm going to get them laminated so Father Time doesn't wreak any more havoc on them." She pushed her glasses up the bridge of her nose.

"Can't you wait for me?" I didn't want Isaac pawing through the recipes while Gramps and I were busy fishing.

"No, I've got it covered." Granny handed Gramps the cooler, walked to the entryway, and called up the stairs. "Isaac, hurry it up, son. Everyone is ready to go."

Figured, Isaac was coming with. I should have known.

He tromped into the room with a beige fisherman's hat stuck on his peanut head. "Ready." I reckoned he couldn't see too well with that hat on, because he narrowly missed bumping into the wall.

"Careful." I grabbed his hand, showing both Granny and Gramps I could act nice. Even be downright hospitable if I so chose.

"Oh, thanks, Maebelle." He pushed the hat up off his eyebrows.

I leaned in to him. "What's wrong with you?"

Isaac stood on his tiptoes and he still couldn't reach my ear. "I took some Dramamine. I didn't want to get seasick. Taking a boat on Lake Michigan always makes me queasy."

I crossed my arms. "Um, Lake Tweedle doesn't empty into the ocean like Lake Michigan. It's not going to be at all choppy."

Isaac gulped. "Now you tell me."

· 10 ·

Little-Known Fact:
Dolphins sleep with one eye
open.

Maybe I should too.

I threaded my worm on the line. I made sure to hook it
twice so the crappie, perch, or walleye that were out there
swimming in the depths of Lake Tweedle wouldn't gobble
up its earthworm breakfast and outsmart me.

"Did you know that a catfish has about a quarter-
million taste buds?" I asked as the little fishing boat
bopped up and down in the wind cutting across the lake.
Gramps wasn't hard of hearing, but the small motor was
loud.

"Is that so?" Gramps asked, cutting the engine. We
neared a narrow stretch of water between two small
patches of land. "And how do you know a thing like that—
from G and T?"

"What's G and T?" Isaac played with his neon green
plastic worm. He wasn't using one of the real ones.

"The Gifted and Talented program," I said. "Lots of schools have them. Robert E. Lee Middle does, where I'm going next year." Of course, right then and there I couldn't admit that I wasn't in G & T anymore, even if I wanted to be.

"Yep, Maebelle's top talent is her no-nonsense noggin." Gramps leaned over and gave me a noogie right on top of my head. "Like yours is the trumpet."

Isaac dropped his plastic worm and held on to the side of the boat. Gramps's moving had swayed it some. Ask me, even with his life jacket on, Isaac was afraid of the water.

"Anyway, I didn't learn about fish taste buds in G and T. I've got this great book I've been reading, Gramps. It is too cool. It has facts on everything: famous people, wars, animals, plants, the body, geography, everything you can think of." I patted my book bag, where I'd stashed the *Little-Known Facts* book, my spiral notebook, my lucky purple pen, and an extra ham biscuit just in case I got super-hungry.

"Here are some other fun fish facts: Most fish don't have eyelids—but sharks do. The tongue of a blue whale can weigh more than the average elephant! And dolphins sleep with one eye open. Wild, huh?"

"Stuff like that only shows up on dumb memorization tests," Isaac said. He was still gripping the side of the boat. He didn't look like he was enjoying himself one bit.

"Tests aren't dumb!" How else were you supposed to know if you were good at something or not, if you weren't tested and graded? "Here's another fact for you: fish don't like plastic worms. You're not going to catch a thing using one of those fake fishing lures."

"Worms are squishy," he said. "And they're alive. Threading them on a hook is gross."

"Squishy, squishy, wormy worm." I dangled a big long earthworm near Isaac's nose. "Isaac's afraid of fishing," I said singsongy.

"Am not."

"Are so," I taunted. I scooched toward him, trying to get the worm closer.

"Hey, now," Gramps warned, but I kept up my pestering.

"Are so!"

"Am not. And I'll show you." Isaac stood on shaky legs and cast out his line. He did it like a pro. Just like Gramps taught me from the banks of the Chattahoochee, that river that Alan Jackson sang about in that "Way Down Yonder" song.

"Who taught you to cast like that?" I asked. Gramps hadn't taken Isaac fishing before today, had he?

"That's for me to know and you to find out," Isaac said.

"Was it your dad?"

Gramps harrumphed, letting me know to knock it off.

"You leave my dad out of this." Isaac objected too. His small shoulders hunched.

"I didn't mean anything by it. I just thought—"

"Kids, hush! I didn't bring the both of you out here so you could scare all the fish away with your jibber-jabbering," Gramps said. "You hear that?"

I breathed in; all I could hear was my heart beating in

my ears. Why wouldn't Isaac talk about his dad? He'd said he was alive. If he was alive, why wasn't Isaac living with him instead of with us?

"I don't hear anything," I said.

"Exactly," said Gramps. "That's Mother Nature's way of talking. To hear her, we just need to button up our yakkers." Gramps kicked off his sandals and set his feet up on one of the benches. "Now, this is what I had in mind. This is what I call taking a breather. . . ."

"Taking a breather," Isaac repeated. "I like the sound of that."

"Yep, just sitting in the sweet silence, me and my two grandkids." Gramps scratched at his chin, his beard whiter than the clouds that dotted the midmorning sky. "And letting it go . . . all of it."

Gramps raised his brows at me when he said that letting-go part, just like Granny had before bed last night. I bet that was his way of telling me not to press Isaac— that he didn't have to talk about his dad or his mom if he didn't want to.

Well, fine. I wasn't trying to be mean. I was just naturally curious.

"After years of playing noisy honky-tonks, this right here"—Gramps gestured to the whole of the lake, and the boat shook with his movements—"is pure heaven."

"Yep, *h-e-a-v-e-n*, heaven," I said, attempting to cast my line. I took my finger off the line too soon. My hook plopped into the water not more than two feet from the boat. Isaac snickered.

This time Gramps raised his brows at him: a sign to stop being so ornery to me.

"Go on, Maebelle, give it another try," Gramps said.

Let it go. Let it go, I told myself. I did my best to pretend Isaac wasn't here. That he was back in Chicago, where I didn't have to see him until Christmas. Or better yet, that he had gone with Aunt Alice to Switzerland and the two of them loved the little cottages, the ice and the snow and the mountains, and had decided they would go there every summer.

This time I took my pointer finger off at the exact right moment, when the pole and my arm were straight out and parallel to the lake.

"Beautiful cast," Gramps said.

"Thanks, Gramps. Practice makes perfect, right?"

"Right."

I listened to my line *click-click-click*ing as it unspooled. I did it. I launched my line way, way, way out. One hundred feet or more and it still hadn't hit the water yet.

Plunk.

I stood to see where my bobber had landed and my foot hit my book bag, tipping me sideways. In one hot second I—*splash!*—fell over the side of the boat and—*smack!*—hit the water.

I plunged under. Lake water went down my throat and up my nose. When I bobbed up, I had lost my pole.

"Maebelle, are you okay?" Gramps asked as I struggled with my life vest. We'd always fished from the shore before.

"I am fine. Fine," I said, spitting out icky lake water.

"That's what I call a belly flop," said Isaac.

"Thanks." My jaw was clenched so tight I barely got the word out. "Maybe I should go out for the Robert E. Lee diving team."

"You'd make it," Isaac said, either not getting my sarcasm or attempting some of his own. "That took some kind of special skill."

Gramps held out his arm. I grabbed near his elbow, and he hauled me over the metal edge of the boat. "There, there, safe and sound." His beard tickled me as he pulled me to him. "Love you, Butter Bean."

He let me go when the boat started to sway again. I kicked my stupid backpack and sat on the floor of the boat, between the bench seats, hugging my knees to my chest. I shivered. It was a warm morning, but the shock of the water and going under like that had given me goose pimples.

"We don't have any towels, do we?" Isaac asked, rooting through the basket Granny had packed.

"Don't think so. We weren't planning on swimming this morning." Gramps took off his Rootin' Tootin' Bootin' Band T-shirt, leaving on his white undershirt. Tufts of gray hair poked out under his arms, but he already had a deep tan. He was browner than the top of a biscuit. "Here you go, Maebelle. You can use this to dry off."

Gramps gave me his shirt and I wiped off my wet arms and legs and then I did my face. I hid in the T-shirt, squeezing out a few tears before using it to absorb the stinky lake water from my hair.

"All better," I said, in between hiccups.

"Nope, sounds like you got the wind knocked out of you. Let's head home." Gramps thumped Isaac's back. "Reel her on in, we've already caught our whopper for the day—isn't that right, Maebelle?"

"Yes, sir," I said, trying not to see the smile that Isaac and Gramps were sharing. That whopper was none other than yours truly.

· 11 ·

Little-Known Fact:
A week before President Lincoln
was shot, he dreamed someone
was crying and mourning over a
coffin at the White House, and
when he asked who had died,
the crying man said President
Lincoln! Lincoln looked in the
coffin and saw himself!

Spooky!

The grimy lake water left me smelling fishier than a can of tuna, but Gramps didn't think bathing in Winnie was a good idea. "These days Winnie needs all her energy just to stay on the road."

I plopped down on one of Winnie's couches, not saying a thing for the entire drive home. When Isaac got up to go to the bathroom, Gramps hollered out: "Lavatory ain't working either."

Isaac settled on the couch next to me. "Sorry I laughed," he said.

"I don't want to talk about it, okay?"

After that, Isaac left me alone. He shifted to the seat opposite me and stared out the window. I wondered if he was thinking about his mom, or his dad, or whoever had taught him to fish.

We were halfway down Azalea Avenue when Oak Alley came into view. I smiled to myself, getting just the slightest bit of satisfaction that the house had a special name, like me. I had tons. And Isaac didn't have a one.

Gramps parked and took his wet T-shirt to the back porch to dry in the sunshine. I trudged upstairs, not even looking for Granny to tell her how terrible fishing had been, and went straight to the bathroom Isaac and I shared. I locked the door that faced Isaac's room so he wouldn't accidentally burst in on me.

I showered, toweled off, and threw on a cotton robe. Then I flung myself on the bed.

"Dream, dream, dream about the closed-off wing," I chanted to myself, hoping that somehow I could forget I had made such a fool out of myself, fall asleep, and dream about where the key to the locked wing was.

•   •   •

I woke with a start. Strings of drool ran from the corner of my mouth to the pillow. I sat up, my head feeling heavy. Had I dreamed about the closed-off wing?

Little-Known Fact: You can make yourself remember your dreams.

I had perfected the technique. I squinched my face real tight as I tried to squeeze dream memories from my nap the way I had wrung lake water from Gramps's T-shirt. Nope. No locked-wing dreams, *aha!*—but I had dreamed something. I smacked my lips. Fruit. I'd dreamed about fruit. Swimming through a river of peaches, strawberries, blackberries, and all manner of fresh fruit fillings. The recipe cards! But why was I dreaming about them?

My stomach rumbled as I hopped out of bed. I reckoned I was just hungry—I hadn't eaten my ham biscuit before my big belly flop, and I hadn't felt like eating it after—but I was more than hungry now. I hurried into my swimsuit, then threw on a clean pair of shorts and a tank top. I almost stopped to call Ruth—I still had her phone number rattling around in my head—to make sure we were still on for swimming, but I didn't. I'd had plenty enough disappointment for one day.

· 12 ·

Little-Known Fact:
Gregory Smith was nominated
for a Nobel Peace Prize when he
was twelve years old.

Me? When I turn twelve, if I don't
get back into Gifted & Talented, I'll
be known as the cousin of Isaac
Johnson, trumpeter extraordinaire.
Yippee.

I rushed downstairs, my hand gliding over the polished railing. I could smell hamburgers, and my growling stomach wanted some—now. I was careful not to let the back porch screen door slam and rattle any of the bells, little figurines, and other porcelain knickknacks that made the bottom floor a kind of old-timey obstacle course.

Gramps must've turned on a jazz station, because whatever song was on was unrecognizable to me. It sure wasn't country. It was happy but mournful at the same time, and even as I was dancing it made me feel sad.

I ducked under the last of the flower baskets that hung from under the porch eaves, and there was Isaac, his trumpet to his lips. The mix of happy-sad notes floated out from it into the hot, humid air. Gramps and Granny sat in the gliding swing with looks of pure contentment on their faces.

"Man." I leaned against the house and slid until I ended up flat on my butt. I folded my long legs up to my chest and listened. The music was strong and pure and wild and contained all at the same time. Isaac's eyes were closed, and his fingers danced across the three valves that changed the notes. I didn't know how he was doing it, since he was the only one playing, but the notes blended together as if a whole jazz quartet was sitting there on the porch.

He held the last note for so long that I got dizzy listening. Sweat glistened on his brow, and when he was finally finished he pulled the trumpet from his mouth and nodded his head. He looked exhausted and excited, as if he had run a marathon. Granny jumped up, clapping and stomping. Gramps followed her lead.

I sat feeling the notes bounce around inside me. No piece of music had ever made me feel like that before, as if I had been running that marathon along with Isaac as he played, not knowing if a hill was coming or a deep valley.

Listening left me breathless.

"Isaac, my, that was something," Granny said. She eyed me. I hadn't been hiding. I was sitting in a daze right out in the open. The way her eyes narrowed, I could tell she was prompting me to say something.

"Yeah, it was." I got up from the porch and dusted my hands off on my knees. That was all I could manage.

"Thanks," Isaac said. "It's a song I've been working on for a while."

"What's it called?" Granny asked as she motioned us all over to the patio table. After thumping Isaac on the back, Gramps sidled over to the grill. Lunch was ready.

"I don't know. I'm not done with it yet. It's about my mom, something she told me before she died."

"Oh, Isaac, what a gift! Music is the perfect way to keep someone with us always," Granny said, wrapping him in her arms. "Your mama was a special woman to raise such a special boy."

"She sure was. Any time you want to talk about her, you go ahead," Gramps said.

Isaac shrugged. "Thanks. I kind of just talk with my music, though."

"That's what makes you a true-blue musician." Gramps dealt the paper plates like they were playing cards. "Alice didn't tell us you were a prodigy—that's what you are, you know? Writing songs at the tender age of ten, and ones that sound like that—whoever heard such a thing!"

Isaac grinned. He soaked up the praise like a pancake soaking up syrup.

· 13 ·

Little-Known Fact:
The one and only William Shakespeare wrote 37 plays and 154 sonnets, which, for those who don't know what a sonnet is (like Isaac—I asked him), is a poem.

But he never wrote anything for the Two-Bit Players.

grabbed a hamburger from the platter and doused it with ketchup and mustard. I took a big honker of a bite, then wished I hadn't. It was overdone—as dry as a hockey puck.

"Oh, Angus," Granny said. "These burgers are burnt." She yanked away the bun and tossed the burger like a Frisbee out into the grass.

"Boo-roo-roo," Cotton barked as he went after the meat. He was tied to a tree, but his leash was long enough for

him to get what he was going after. He ate greedily, making snuffling sounds as he chomped.

Granny crunched a pickle. "You better not enter the blue-ribbon burger contest at the Anniversary Spectacular."

"Anniversary Spectacular?" I swallowed—gulped, more like it—to get the dry meat down. "What's that?"

"Tweedle is having a big party for the town's hundred and seventy-fifth anniversary," said Isaac.

I plunked my elbows on the tabletop. I didn't care if it was bad manners. "So how do you know about it?"

"Life doesn't stop when you're napping," Isaac said between mouthfuls. He was the only one eating his burger with any gusto.

"Did you sneak into my room?"

"I did no such thing," he said. "Granny sent me to get you to see if you wanted to go with us, but I could hear you snoring out in the hallway."

"Fine. Fine," I said. Ranjeet had told me I snored at her last slumber party. She said I sounded like a bear—how embarrassing. "So where did you go? What did I miss?"

Granny plopped another dill pickle in her mouth and took a swig of her lemonade. "I steamed apart those recipe cards. What a find, Maebelle! I can't wait to cook something from them."

"*And...*," I prompted Granny, wondering what the recipe cards had to do with this Anniversary Spectacular thing.

"Well, Isaac tagged along with me when I hoofed it

over to Fred's Five-and-Dime. I figured if any place in town had a laminating machine it would be the five-and-dime. They blow up balloons for birthdays and sell all sorts of stuff—"

"And . . . ," I interrupted again.

"While we were waiting in line, Mrs. Mayor—"

"Eliza Fitzwhelm," said Isaac, in a fake Southern drawl. He took a spare paper plate and fanned himself, imitating the mayor, I guess.

"Right, Mrs. Mayor Eliza Fitzwhelm is how she introduced herself, and she said"—Granny started talking as if she had a corncob suddenly stuck up her nose—"'My, my, I have been meaning to pop over to say hello. Edith Eberlee, the old prune—and I do mean no disrespect, God rest her soul—never was one for entertaining, but I suppose the invitations will now be a-coming, since you and your husband are show people. Are y'all opening the west wing?'"

Gramps shifted in his seat at the mention of the locked wing, but my ears pricked up.

"'Rumor has it that was the private quarters of Josiah T. Eberlee, who was good friends with General Turner, imagine that. Perhaps there is something in the locked wing that we could put on display at the Anniversary Spectacular. Wouldn't that be something!'"

The mayor lady had mentioned Josiah T., the name I'd seen in the guest ledger!

Before I could ask any questions, Granny stood. She was getting into this playacting. "Isaac, c'mon, you be me."

Isaac hopped up; he didn't need any more prompting.

"And Granny said"—he lowered his chin and tried to muster up Granny's deep voice—"'True, true, but we are retired entertainers now, and my husband, Angus T., is going to abide by old Edith's wishes. The west wing shall remain shut forever.'"

Please. Isaac sounded nothing like Granny.

Granny swung her arm up to her forehead, in full swoon, making the mayor out to be a bit on the dramatic side. "'Say 'tisn't so. But not to even peek into the wing . . . and never to play again?'"

Isaac copied Granny's toe-tapping move. "'We play in our backyard. I do hope none of the neighbors have complained to the town council.'"

I snorted. "Granny would never sound so formal," I said.

They ignored me.

I crossed my arms over my chest. Even in playacting I was a stickler.

"'Oh, no, dear heart,'" Granny said, back in her Mrs. Mayor role. "'Don't trouble yourself at all fretting about that. Not a soul has complained. We are all curious about what talents you show folks will bring to the table.'"

Granny snapped up the paper plate Isaac had been using as a fan and began waving it around herself. "'In fact, I hereby cordially invite y'all, right here, right now, to be the main attraction at the Town of Tweedle's One Hundred and Seventy-fifth Anniversary Spectacular! You must play for us, you must.'"

"'I wish we could, but the Rootin' Tootin' Bootin' Band is did, done, and over with,'" Isaac said, using one of

Granny's favorite phrases. He squinched his lips together, which sometimes Granny did when she wanted to look sad but was secretly happy.

"'What about playing under another name?'"

"'Oh, that could work,'" Isaac said, as Granny. "'Isaac, any ideas?'"

Isaac swung his body around and now pretended to be none other than himself. "'Oh, I got one! How about . . . the Eberlee Explosion?'"

"'Exciting, alliterative,'" said Mrs. Mayor, aka Granny.

Isaac shifted his stance and stuck out his hip, back to being Granny. "'Perfect, Li'l Bit, perfect.'"

I almost bit my tongue. Isaac had been given his own nickname, *Li'l Bit*? I would have voted for Peanut Head.

Isaac went on with his Granny impersonation. "'Then you have to play with us. If we are going to be known as the Explosion, then we'll need you on trumpet backing us up!'"

He turned again. I was getting dizzy. Was Gramps following all this?

"'Why, of course, I, Isaac "Li'l Bit" Johnson, would be happy to play with the Eberlee Explosion!'"

Perfect! Li'l Bit had all the luck.

"'Then it's settled—the Eberlee Explosion will be billed as our main attraction.'" Granny was getting good at her impression. "'This year's Anniversary Spectacular is going to be spectacular indeed!'"

Granny flung out her arms. Isaac did the same. They bowed low and long, like they were actors bound for

Broadway. Thank heavens, the Two-Bit Players were done. They were giving me a headache.

"My, my, I didn't know there was such a thing as lunch theater," said Gramps. "I look forward to playing at the—what was it called?"

"The Town of Tweedle's One Hundred and Seventy-fifth Anniversary Spectacular," I said.

"How long do we have for rehearsals?" Gramps asked.

"Close to three weeks," answered Isaac.

I sat swinging my feet for a second, waiting to be included—even Mama and Daddy allowed me to be their sound-check girl—but the conversation kept chug-chug-chugging along. Eventually, I pushed away from the table and sauntered over to Cotton and untied him.

"We should write some new songs," Gramps was saying to Granny. "I'm not sure we can use Isaac in 'Either You or Your Dog Done Given Me Fleas.'"

"How about this? What if we jazz up the country songs and country up some jazz standards?" offered Isaac.

"Oh, sounds good," said Granny. "Now, for costumes, it's sure to be hot, but I still think we need a little razzle-dazzle."

I tugged on Cotton's leash and he came trailing after me. We went around to the side porch, where there was another entrance to the house. I'd grab an apple and a string cheese or two inside. No one called after me to remind me that I hadn't excused myself or that I hadn't helped clear. They were too busy dreaming up all the ways the Eberlee Explosion could explode onto the scene.

· 14 ·

Little-Known Fact:
Dogs can be identified by their nose prints, just like humans can be identified by their fingerprints.

I hope Cotton never gets dog-napped or goes missing. I love "that dog," as Isaac calls him, and he loves me.

Even though I'd only arrived twenty-four hours ago, it felt like eons had passed. Ruth had better not have forgotten about her afternoon swimming-hole invite. Diving and jumping and having fun with someone other than Isaac was exactly what I needed. I stuffed a beach towel and some sunscreen in my backpack and left a note on the counter telling the Eberlee Explosion where I'd gone off to, in case they cared.

"C'mon, boy, let's get out of here." There was no reason Cotton should have been stuck sleeping under a shade tree. His belly was big enough as it was, dragging almost to the ground, like his ears. He needed the exercise and I needed the company.

Cotton wandered out from the laundry room and I clipped a leash onto his collar and we snuck off, letting the party go on without us.

Cotton and I trudged this way and that, turning left and right on streets we'd never been down before in search of the swimming hole. I didn't care if I got lost. I just wanted *away*, as in *far, far away*. Cotton and I turned a corner and I found that we'd ended up on Main, smack-dab in front of the Georgia Peach depot.

Giles waved and then hollered, "Hi, Miss Maebelle, how're you? Liking life here in Tweedle?"

"Not really," I muttered before clearing my throat to speak louder. "I mean, yes, sir, I'm liking it fine."

I kept walking and then I backtracked. I went right up to Giles where he was washing the depot windows, waiting on the next bus to pass through, and said: "Isaac's adopted, just so you know."

"Is that so?" asked Giles. The corners of his mouth turned up, as if he wanted to laugh or at least chuckle.

"Yes, that is so!" I said. Sure, I didn't like Isaac hogging all the attention, but I didn't think it was right that someone gave him weird looks just because he was black. "But for your information, even though he's not blood kin, he could be. There's nothing wrong with people who don't look alike marrying and having babies."

"I didn't say there was," said Giles. He was still standing there smirking. I wasn't trying to be amusing, so what was so funny?

"Are you laughing at me?" I asked, and then since I didn't want to be accused of back-talking an elder, I threw in a "sir" for good measure.

"No, no," Giles said. "I'm smiling because my wife is African American and pregnant, and I was glad to see a kid like Isaac fitting in so well. I didn't mean to stare."

"Good, I'm glad you weren't giving my family funny looks yesterday on purpose." I was as bad as Granny was at not getting to the point. I was as jazzed on the inside as a shaken Coca-Cola. I wasn't making a lick of sense. I took a deep breath.

"Cotton and I are on our way to the swimming hole, but we don't know where it is. Can you point us in the right direction?"

"First, go thataway." Giles pointed to the center of town. There was a bandstand there. Or a gazebo or something. Whatever it was, it was circular and looked like a gathering place. That was probably where the Eberlee Explosion was going to play.

"And once you cut through Tweedle Park you're only a hop, skip, and a jump away. Just keep walking until you hit the Kiss-Me-Quick Bridge."

"Kiss-Me-Quick Bridge?" I asked.

"Oh, how about that! You don't know, do you?" Giles slapped his knee and Cotton barked like he would be getting a treat. I yanked his leash a tiny bit so he wouldn't go smelling Giles in places where he shouldn't. "That bridge got that name because Josiah T. Eberlee"—my ears pricked up. Here was his name again!—"was quite the ladies' man. Town legend has it that he'd come to call on a young lady and ask to take her for a walk, when the only thing he had his sights set on was getting her far enough away from her chaperone to get a quick kiss. He'd sneak one day or night, if he could get away with it."

"Are you telling me he used the bridge as his special make-out spot?"

"I sure am." Giles hadn't stopped scrubbing the whole time he was giving his local history lesson, but now he stopped and turned to me. "Is that why you're headed to the swimming hole? To go consorting with a boy?"

"N-o. The only boy here I know is Isaac, and I wouldn't kiss him if he were the very last boy on the planet." My face puckered as if I was sucking a lemon.

Giles laughed at that. "If I recall, he was all gentlemanly, picking up your book for you and everything. Maybe he's sweet on you? I was about his age when I got my first girlfriend."

"Ha, ha, you're a funny guy, Giles," I said, taking off in the direction he'd sent me. Cotton's collar jingled as we strolled. I walked backward, getting in the last word: "But don't even joke about such a thing. Isaac and I aren't *really* related, but we *are* related, you know."

I shuddered. Kiss Isaac! *G-r-o-s-s*, gross!

· 15 ·

Little-Known Fact:
There is an actual song titled
"Aunt Jemima and Your Uncle
Cream of Wheat." It was written
in 1936 by Johnny Mercer and
Rube Bloom.

I almost wrote my own song:
"Cousin Isaac, the Ruiner of
Summer Vacations."

Out in the muddy water, Ruth was floating on her
back as if she didn't have a care in the world. I saw
her a ways away, her nose sticking out of the water and her
hair floating around her as if she were Medusa, the ancient
Greek who turned soldiers to stone with one look at her
and her snake hair.

I hollered, "Hey, Ruth, I'm here! Found you!"

"Maebelle!" Ruth flipped herself underwater and then
swam my way. When she came up for air, she continued as

if she had never stopped talking. "I knew you would! You're psychic, remember?"

"How could I forget?"

But I had forgotten. Would she like me if I told the truth now? That I was the furthest thing from a know-it-all swami as could be? I didn't want to take that chance, so I kept my lips zipped.

"Well, what are you waiting for? C'mon in, the water's fine," she said. "It's just us and those little kids over there." She pointed to the far side of the swimming hole, where a group of toddlers with floaties on their arms were playing with their moms. "But no boys. Not even any frogs to kiss."

"Good! I'm sick of boys."

I got goose pimples as I ran across the Kiss-Me-Quick Bridge. This was the very same bridge where Josiah T. had kissed all those bonneted Southern belles over a century ago! And if the locked wing had been his personal quarters, I just had to get in there!

Cotton trotted by my side. His paws made a *ting-ting-ting* sound as they hit the creaky old wood. I'd find out more about Josiah T. later. Right now, I was going to have fun and forget about my family—both its older and newer members.

"I'm going to dump my stuff over here," I called.

I walked over to where Ruth's flip-flops and other stuff were spread out under a tall tree. A sign on a plank of wood read SWIM AT YOUR OWN RISK.

I read it and agreed. I'd risk anything to be away from Isaac right then.

I dumped my book bag and shimmied out of my clothes. I wasn't a great swimmer, but I had taken a few classes at the Y. I snapped on my goggles and gathered Cotton into my arms.

"Ready or not, here we come." I waded in, letting the sandy, muddy mush of the bottom ooze between my toes. I went out deeper and deeper, clutching Cotton to me as if he was a pool noodle that could keep me afloat. The lukewarm water neared my waist. Cotton *boo-roo-roo*ed and wiggled out of my arms, wanting to be free. He doggy-paddled straight to Ruth and began licking her face.

"What's his name?" Ruth asked, raising her chin.

"Cotton."

The sun was so hot on the top of my head it was starting to feel like I could fry an egg up there. I dunked under the water and swam a bit. When I popped to the surface, Ruth was still cooing and ooing over Cotton.

"He is the cutest, cutest thing. I've got a Lab back home. Why didn't you tell me you had a dog?" Ruth asked.

"She doesn't," said Isaac, from the tree where I had just dumped my stuff.

What was *he* doing here?

"Cotton is our grandparents' dog."

"Oh, my gosh," Ruth squealed. "Are you Maebelle's brother? Maebelle, you didn't tell me you had a brother."

"He is not my brother!" I shouted. My voice echoed under the bridge. *Not . . . not . . . not.* "This here is Isaac. He's my cousin from Chicago. And he was just leaving," I added.

"I was?"

"You were." I stomped out of the water in full-fledged boss mode. "Do Granny and Gramps know where you've run off to?"

"They're not worried—not about me," Isaac said, a smile creeping across his face. "They were worried about you until I found your note."

"Ah, you found it. Good for you."

"What does that mean?" Isaac asked.

"Nothing, never mind."

"You two coming swimming or what?" Ruth called. "With three of us we can play Marco Polo."

Was Ruth *that* boy-crazy? Isaac wasn't a boy . . . he was Isaac.

She plugged her nose and then dove under the surface. When she came up she had her eyes closed and said: "Marco!"

"Polo," answered Isaac. Then he turned to me. "I've always wanted to play Marco Polo. Can I stay? Pretty please?"

"You've never played Marco Polo?"

"I was always at the hospital—with my mom. Please?" He looked at me with sad puppy-dog eyes, sadder than Cotton's.

How on earth could I say no?

"All right," I snarled. "But Ruth thinks I'm a psychic, so don't go blowing my cover."

"A psychic?"

"Don't ask," I said. "It's too long to explain."

"Okay, you're a psychic. Whatever," he said. "As long as I can stay."

"Yep, go ahead, play Marco Polo until the cows come home."

"Really?" Isaac threw his arms around me and hugged me hard. "Cool, Maebelle. You're the best, cuz."

He kicked off his sandals. Then he took off his T-shirt. He'd come prepared. All he had left on were his swimming trunks.

"Duck and cover," he yelled as he trotted around the tree doing some weird gallop, and then beelined it for the rocky, sandy drop-off, where he jumped and curled into a ball, which wasn't hard since he was snail-sized. He hit the water as Ruth ducked, hiding behind her arm while a wave flew into the air.

"The judge from Chattanooga, Tennessee," Ruth hollered as Cotton swam around in circles, "gives that dive a perfect ten!"

· 16 ·

Little-Known Fact:
In 1872 a dentist named Mahlon
Loomis applied for and was
granted a patent for wireless
telegraphy, but today Nikola Tesla
is considered the inventor
of the radio.

No wonder hearing the
announcement of the Marvelous
Main Attraction felt like getting a
cavity filled.

The clock radio on my bedside table went off. I had set
the alarm for 9:00 a.m. on the dot.

"Good morning, town of Tweedle. Mother Nature is serving up a hot-plate special today—the temperature is fixin' to get to the high nineties—and she is also serving up a side helping of HUMID. Look for sporadic thunder boomers to put a damper on any outdoor plans. No fishing. No swimming.

No paddle boating, as lightning and thunder are expected to rattle and shake."

I covered my face with my pillow. We'd had fun yesterday at the swimming hole, dunking each other and doing underwater somersaults. Isaac wasn't half bad if I got him away from all the pancake-syrup praise Granny and Gramps heaped on him, but I knew if I was stuck inside with him all day I'd hear nothing but "Isaac this" and "Isaac that."

The deejay's spiel went on.

"But though the day may be a wash, I've got some good news. Mrs. Mayor Fitzwhelm called in to WKIT over the last commercial break, and she wanted me to let all my listeners know that if you weren't already excited about the Town of Tweedle's Hundred and Seventy-fifth Anniversary Spectacular, well, then get ready. . . . She tells it best herself . . . let me roll the tape!"

I sat up in bed and listened closely. A new voice came on, and even with the fiddle music playing in the background I could tell Granny had a knack for voices. Her impersonation of Mrs. Mayor had been dead-on.

"Tweedle knights and Tweedle ladies, this year's Anniversary Spectacular is going to be more spectacular than ever. First off, blue ribbons this year will be awarded in the following categories: In the cooking competitions we have Best Burger, Most Delicious Dessert, Tastiest Chili, and Most Fabulous Fried Fritter. Overall competitions are Best Hog in Show, Chicken Chasing, Mutton Bustin', Town of Tweedle's Biggest Tomato, and Best Homemade Crafts and Other Tweedle Trinkets.

"The usual highlight of the Anniversary Spectacular, the

kids' dance competition, will of course take place, but unlike in years past, when the awards were based on applause, this year we have Trina Von Decker in from Atlanta to judge the competition! Her results will be announced after the MARVELOUS MAIN ATTRACTION.

"*That's right, my beloved constituents, the gazebo in the center of town is going to be repainted, and in it, the heirs to Oak Alley, the oldest home in Tweedle, will treat the town to a rootin' tootin' concert. . . . That's right, folks, Angus T. and Ivory Ann Eberlee, along with their grandson, Isaac 'Li'l Bit' Johnson, are going to take the stage, and all among us will witness the birth of the Eberlee Explosion—so grab your rockabilly boots and your shadiest sun hat and get ready for an Anniversary Spectacular that will beat all others!*"

The radio switched back to the deep-voiced deejay:

"*That's right, folks. You heard it here on WKIT. For further information and contest rules, be sure to read this morning's* Tweedle Gazette.

"*And now back to the music. Here's an old ditty from a fella who should have known when to hold 'em and when to fold 'em when it came to the plastic surgery: Kenny Rogers, singing 'Coward of the County.'*"

I hit the Off button. I had heard enough.

· 17 ·

Little-Known Fact:
The handheld BlackBerry
device got its name because
the buttons on it looked like
little seeds.

Mama and Daddy never let their
BlackBerries out of their sight.

The list of contests Mrs. Mayor announced on the radio was so long I could barely remember any of it. I shoved on some clothes and ran to the driveway. I snuck back inside with the *Tweedle Gazette* and spread it out at the kitchen table. Yes, sir, I wanted one of those blue ribbons. I *needed* one of those blue ribbons!

I read over all the rules and regulations and flat-out decided against competing for Best Hog in Show, since (a) I didn't have a hog, (b) I'd never go near it if I did have one, and (c) even if I did, I wouldn't want to risk my pig coming in last place.

Another option was Mutton Bustin'. A judge timed

kids to see who could sit on a sheep the longest without falling off. I totally thought I would excel at that, but Granny, who came into the kitchen to get her morning coffee brewing, pointed out that the contest was only for kids six and under. Shoot.

The Chicken Chasing contest sounded lame. I didn't have time to grow the town of Tweedle's biggest tomato and I had no knack for crafts, so all that was left were the cooking contests.

"Granny, where are those Eberlee family recipe cards I found?" I asked, staring at the rules for the Most Delicious Dessert contest.

"I put them in the hutch in the dining room."

"Why there?" I asked.

Granny tweaked my nose. "'Cause my Tater Tot uncovered 'em. And that's where I found some other family heirlooms."

"Oh, wow. I want to see."

Granny led me to the hutch, which was big and heavy, with wooden doors. She undid the latches and opened one of the cabinets.

"See, there's the family Bible. I hoped it would have a family tree inside, but it doesn't."

I set the Bible on the dining room table. "What else did you find?"

"Some fancy china, passed on from more nameless, faceless folk. But oh, goodness." Granny clapped her hands together. "I found a silver tankard. I had to polish it up. It was way in the back, tarnished and long forgotten."

Granny took the polished tankard out of the hutch.

The silver glinted in the light streaming through the dining room windows. It sure didn't look to me like storms were coming. "Is there writing on it?" I asked.

"There sure is." Granny handed me the tankard. I traced the engraved words with my finger and then I read them out loud: "*For Josiah T., With my admiration and friendship always, Charles Turner.* Isn't that the guy on the town welcome sign?" I held the tankard. It was cool and shiny.

"It sure is. I called the mayor and told her about it, and it's going to be on display at the Anniversary Spectacular."

I smiled but my gut fell. Even an old tin cup was going to shine brighter than me at the big shindig.

I glanced over my shoulder and made sure neither Isaac nor Gramps was around. "Didn't the mayor say the locked wing was once Josiah T.'s private quarters?"

"That she did. When Isaac and I were at the five-and-dime."

"Then what is the tankard doing out here?" I asked. "And what do you think Josiah T. did to deserve it?"

"Not sure," Granny said. "You know, doctors and lawyers back then often had their offices in their homes. Maybe the locked wing was Josiah T.'s office? He could have been a doctor or a lawyer. Helping General Turner with a health crisis or a legal jam might have earned him the tankard."

"Maybe, but the only kind of work I heard Josiah did was smooch-smooch-smooching." I made fish lips.

Granny's brows arched as she laughed at my kissy-face face. "I see you've been doing some investigating on your own," she said.

"Giles from the bus station told me the Kiss-Me-

Quick Bridge in town was named after Josiah 'cause he took all the girls there for unchaperoned kisses."

"Ha! Now I know where your gramps got his luck with the ladies. His charm must be hereditary." Granny took the mug from me and placed it back in the hutch. She whispered in my ear, "Speaking of my one great love, I know I told your grandfather I was fine honoring old Edith's wishes, but my curiosity is killing me." She nodded her head toward the west wing. "I've just got to get in there. I've been searching high and low for the key ever since you found those recipes. What if there really is something we can take to *Antiques Roadshow*?"

Her eyes twinkled. I liked knowing she was up to something. The same something I wanted to be up to.

"Oh, Granny!" I laughed. "You're baaaaad."

"Now, don't tell a soul. Your gramps would have my hide. I've asked him again about opening that letter Edith left him, but he won't budge. He told me he put it in a safe-deposit box at the bank."

"He doesn't trust us?" I asked.

Granny giggled. "Of course not, he's a smart man."

I giggled too. It was fun to be sharing secrets with Granny.

"I'll keep my lips zipped," I said, "on one condition."

Granny placed her hands on her hips. "What's that?"

"That if and when you get in, I get to explore with you. I already found the recipe cards and I've got a good eye."

"That you do." Granny reached into one of the hutch drawers and slapped the recipe cards into the palm of my hand. "You drive a hard bargain, Turnip Toes."

She marched me back to the kitchen. But I didn't stay there for long. The recipe card on top of the stack sounded like a blue-ribbon winner. I grabbed a plastic pail and headed outside. There were blackberries just waiting to be picked.

· 18 ·

Little-Known Fact:
The world's most poisonous
mushroom is the *Amanita
phalloides,* which is known as
the death cap!

I sure hope blackberries aren't
poisonous.

I read Cotton the ingredients on the laminated card as we headed away from the house and deep into the woods, to a parcel of land that surely must've been part of the Eberlee property at some point. I eyed the recipe card. The handwriting was barely legible; it was shaky, kind of like a first grader's or someone just learning to write. Not fancy-schmancy like the script in the Oak Alley guest ledger.

"So, Cotton, get a load of this. These are the ingredients we need from the old Eberlee family recipe: six big handfuls of blackberries from the bushes near the creek, three-quarters cup of sugar, three pinches of flour, one-half cup of well water, some fresh-squeezed lemon juice, and three pats of butter.

"And for the crumbles: two cups of flour, a few pinches of sugar, a small pinch of salt, one-half cup of buttermilk, one-quarter teaspoon of baking soda, and as much lard as needed. And it's signed 'Hannah V.'"

Cotton breathed heavily in-out, in-out. I reckoned he was in full agreement with every last word I read.

"Yeah, sounds like Hannah V. Eberlee knew what she was talking about." I flipped the card over. The second half of the recipe, the instructions part, was missing, but how hard could it be? Especially since my long-lost relation had told me where to pick the juiciest blackberries around. I hadn't seen the creek bed for myself, but Gramps had told Isaac and me where it was on the way home from our fishing fiasco.

We walked on, maybe only four or five hundred feet more, it was hard to tell, because there wasn't really a path. I didn't want any burrs or brambles or anything to get stuck on Cotton's coat, and then I saw the little creek snaking through the trees. There was a row of dilapidated stone buildings—warehouses for crops, maybe. Vines grew in and out and around them. Up on the hill above them was a brick chimney—the rest of that house must have been destroyed over the years.

I slapped my leg. "This way, boy, I think we've found it! We've got to hurry, it's supposed to rain."

Cotton, as old as he was, still had some pep in his step. He stuck his nose low to the ground and sniff-sniff-

sniffed his way through a bunch of weeds and scraggly grass as I made my way over to a mess of blackberry bushes. He followed me, his snout to the ground. I pretended he had discovered the bushes. "Good job, Cotton!" I clapped. Even a dog needed praise.

I grabbed a bunch of the berries. The day was hot and sticky, just like that radio deejay had said, and the fruit was warm. The berries were so full of juice I thought they might pop out of their blackberry skins. I laid them as gently as I could in the bucket.

I slid one into my mouth; it was . . . better than good, but I didn't have the word for it. The blackberry, I decided, was indescribable.

· · ·

I had just about collected what I'd figured was enough berries to fill a large square baking pan when the breeze picked up. It smelled like the morning before, wet and humid and dewy, and now it felt thick with the coming rain. Thunder clapped, and seconds later lightning shot through the sky. Cotton took off running. The WKIT weatherman had been right: a big storm was coming.

According to my *Little-Known Facts* book, there were thirty lightning flashes occurring all over the world at any given second. What if city boy Isaac was sitting in one of those old oak trees, playing his trumpet, like he had been yesterday?

"Run, Cotton, run! We've got to save Isaac!" We hightailed it, running as fast as we could while I tried not to spill any berries from the bucket.

· 19 ·

Little-Known Fact:
No kid has ever won the
Pillsbury Bake-Off. That's
because the rules say you have
to be over eighteen to enter.

Sounds like ageism—which Granny
complained some honky-tonk
owners have—to me.

closed my eyes. I could hear it: the hush falling over the crowd as the winner of the Most Delicious Dessert contest was announced.

"And the prize goes to the town's newest and brightest culinary star. Miss Mouthwaterin' Maebelle Earl for her scrum-delicious, crumb-crumbiest blackberry cobbler. Come on down, blue-ribbon baker!" I imagined a voice saying. The crowd would cheer as I ran from the bleachers and went onstage to collect my ribbon. Gramps would call out, "That's my girl, my one and only!"

That big moment would be followed by another—me

shyly grinning and blinking through my bangs for the *Tweedle Gazette* photographer. When the story ran in the paper, Granny would clip it out and stick it up on the fridge. Everyone would be in awe, even Isaac. "I never knew you could bake like that," he'd say. "It makes me want to write a song."

"I don't need a song. My baking makes its own mouth-watering music."

Yep, that was exactly the way it would go down.

I tapped my pocket. The key to my success was right there.

The berries I had collected were waiting for me in the back of the pantry, hidden in the bucket, with a paper towel draped over them. While I'd been waiting for the thundershowers to pass, I'd checked to make sure we had the rest of the ingredients. I needed to get buttermilk and lard.

When the rain settled to a drizzle, I nabbed an umbrella from the bronze can in the corner of the foyer.

"Going out for a stroll," I called, trying to get out the front door before anyone stopped me.

"Hold it," Gramps called out. "Not so fast."

Ugh. I trudged to where Granny, Gramps, and Isaac were sitting around the parlor table playing Scrabble. I wasn't one hundred percent sure what made it a parlor and not a living room, but I thought it had to do with the heavy blue chintz curtains.

"Are you going to see Ruth? Can I come?" asked Isaac.

"No and no." My nose crinkled.

"Maebelle?" Gramps pushed up his bifocals with his pointer finger.

"What? Isaac's in the middle of a game. It would be rude for me to interrupt."

Granny gave me the evil eye. It was the exact same look I'd gotten when I'd melted Mama's Ruby Red lipstick and used it for the lava to come out of the Mount St. Helens replica I made for a G & T project.

"I won't be long. Y'all have to rehearse soon anyway— they announced the Eberlee Explosion on the radio this morning, so you've got to be good. The whole town is coming. And when you're done, I'm going to have a surprise for you. So really *no one* can go with me."

"Well, you're not leaving this house unless you tell us where you're going, surprise or not," Gramps said.

"Fine." I cupped my hand and whispered into his hairy ear: "The market."

"Why?" Gramps asked. Again, I kept my voice as hush-hush as humanly possible: "I am making a special dessert for tonight's supper from one of those recipe cards. I got spending money from Mama and Daddy before they left. I want to use some on the surprise. It'll be good. I promise." I patted Gramps's belly. As flat as it was, he did have a sweet tooth—an incurable one, Granny said.

"She can go." Gramps picked up a Scrabble tile and went back to playing his game. "But don't go anywhere else, and come right back. Tweedle isn't Atlanta, but I won't have your mother complaining that we let you run wild when she calls tonight."

I kissed Gramps's whiskery cheek. "Thanks! Be back in a bit!"

"Wait, what's the surprise?" Isaac stood and jarred

the Scrabble board. The tiles moved off their squares. The game was ruined; they'd have to start over.

"That's for me to know and you to find out." I gave him a self-satisfied smile and was *g-o-n-e,* gone, before Gramps could change his mind.

· 20 ·

Little-Known Fact:
Humans eat about sixty thousand
pounds of food in a lifetime.
That's more than what six
elephants weigh!

Half of Gramps's intake must
be made up of cakes, cookies,
and pies. That man sure has a
sweet tooth.

The kitchen was a *w-r-e-c-k*, wreck. Bluish black
blackberry bits clung to the stovetop, splashed from
the saucepan where I'd brought the sugar and berries to a
boil. Once the boiling was done, I poured the berry mix-
ture into a pan and spooned the dough stuff over the top
for the crumbly topping. The whole time, I kept watch
out the closed window (I'd turned the AC on high since I
was cooking) to make sure Isaac didn't get any bright

ideas and run into the house for a glass of water or anything.

But Gramps kept everyone fully hydrated out there in the shade under the large oak by dragging out the old Rootin' Tootin' Bootin' Band cooler. I set the oven timer for forty-five minutes and then I raced around the kitchen, sponge in hand, trying to scrub up my mess.

Outside, Granny had stopped singing and Gramps had stopped playing his acoustic guitar. Isaac was practicing his horn solo. It scared the bejeepers out of me every time he let loose with a wail. I dropped my sponge more times than I could count. Granny had said she was glad to have a real kitchen now—especially after all those years cooking on the tiny hot plate in Winnie. And I wasn't in the mood to hear a lecture if I missed one blackberry splotch. Not in front of Gramps, and especially not in front of Isaac.

The kitchen buzzer was counting down and I was drying off the last of the dishes when Granny and Gramps walked in. They headed straight for the paper towels to wipe their sweaty faces and necks.

"So what did you make?" Isaac asked, sniffing around. "Gramps spilled that it's a dessert, and it sure smells good, so what is it?"

"Gramps! How could you?"

"Isaac twisted my arm. He refused to rehearse until I told him what I knew." Gramps unhooked his guitar from the shoulder strap he wore and set it in its case. "You forgive me, don't you?"

I stood guard in front of the oven. "Maybe, maybe not.

I'm not sure you deserve a piece of my scrum-delicious . . ." I waited a beat, deciding if I would tell what it was or make them wait until after dinner. ". . . crumb-crumbiest . . . blackberry cobbler."

"Yum!" Gramps tossed his paper towel toward the trash can. It hit the rim and went in. "I love cobbler."

"Me too." Granny ruffled my hair, messing up my bangs as she sniffed at the air. The cobbler's sugary sweetness clung to it thickly, like the Spanish moss that grew in trees. "I was all set to suggest we eat dessert first just to find out what special recipe you were making, but that was before the Hillibrands next door asked us over. They've got two boys, Jimmy and Taylor—both are close in age to you and Isaac—and a baby girl, Savannah, about six months old."

Isaac bounced on his tiptoes. "And surprise! We're bringing dessert."

I hadn't planned on serving my very first cobbler to strangers. I wanted to unveil the recipe to family only.

"Great," I said, even though it was the opposite of the way I felt.

"Good, dinner is in ten. Go wash up," Granny instructed. "We don't want to be late."

• • •

A dark-skinned kid with short hair, the same cut as Isaac's, answered the Hillibrands' door.

"MOM, the guests are here! Hey there. You must be Isaac." He stuck out his hand like he was a politician. Isaac shook it. "And you must be Maebelle." He thumped me on the back.

"Watch out," I said. "This is hot." I held the cobbler away from my body. I'd wrapped it in tinfoil, and I didn't want to drop it.

The boy was regular-sized—not extra-tall like me or extra shrimpy like Isaac—so I wasn't sure if he was the older or the younger Hillibrand. He said hello to Granny and Gramps and everyone started gabbing at once, right there in the doorway.

"Hey." I held the pan out. "Where can I put this? It's getting heavy."

Granny started to object to my manners, but the boy pointed me toward the kitchen. "Go right in there. C'mon, I'll show you my room." He tugged Isaac away. "Maebelle, we'll be up here."

They climbed the stairs to the second floor. Another boy stuck his head into the upstairs hallway, the sound of a television or a computer behind him. "Hi, I'm Taylor," he said. "So cool that you're here. Want to play Crash 'Em and Dash 'Em?"

"Awesome," Isaac said. "Next door we don't even have a TV."

I waited for Isaac to invite me along—especially since I had let him swim with Ruth and me—but he didn't. He didn't even turn around to see if I was okay hanging out all alone with the adults and baby Savannah, who was conked out sleeping in her swingy chair.

I dropped off my cobbler in the kitchen as all the adults

talked and took seats, and then I did what I did at all of Mama and Daddy's parties when I was the only kid around: I dug out my book and got to reading.

Little-Known Fact: The anteater is a solitary mammal. It keeps company with other anteaters only when mating and when taking care of its young.

Little-Known Fact:
Boston is nicknamed Beantown
because of Boston Baked Beans.

The side dish, not the icky candy
that used to give me gas every
Halloween. I sure hope the
Hillibrands aren't serving anything
fart-worthy.

When we were all ushered into the dining room, I
ended up having to sit next to Taylor, who at thirteen was the older brother of Jimmy, the boy who had
answered the door. I pulled my chair closer to Gramps,
who was on my other side. I hated dumb boys who
thought girls couldn't hang and do boy stuff: Play video
games. Race bikes. Play kickball.

Isaac sat between Jimmy and Taylor, and he looked
as pleased as punch with his new buddies. They kept
snickering and making Crash 'Em and Dash 'Em noises,
until Mrs. Hillibrand nicely asked them to hush.

After we all said grace, Mr. Hillibrand uncovered the casserole dish.

I stared into the dish—in it floated some gray-purplish goop.

"We hope you don't mind, we're vegetarians," said Mr. Hillibrand.

"Our spicy eggplant is wonderful, though. The boys love it." Mrs. Hillibrand was busy filling up water glasses while Mr. Hillibrand dished out the brown rice and eggplant. Savannah had woken up and was sitting in a high chair. Lucky her—she got strained carrots and some banana baby food for dinner.

"Well, I love my ribs," Gramps said, "but a little something new never killed me. At least not yet." Everyone laughed.

"Gramps is an omnivore," I said, wondering if Taylor and Jimmy even knew what an omnivore was. "We all are. Even Isaac. That means we eat plants and animals."

"Oh, neat," said Taylor.

"How'd you know that?" asked Jimmy.

"I told you," said Isaac. "Maebelle's got a good memory."

I sat up straighter. The boys had been talking about me? Good. "That I do."

Dinner began in earnest. The Hillibrand boys shoveled food in like hungry football players. Isaac had thirds of that disgusting goop. I ate an entire plateful—more brown rice than anything else, but I was worried that if I didn't clean my plate I wasn't going to get any dessert.

The conversation was typical getting-to-know-the-neighbors stuff. At one point Mrs. Hillibrand turned to

Gramps. "So, what kind of relationship did you have with your aunt? The boys and I made Christmas cookies each December for her, but she never once invited us in."

Jimmy grumbled under his breath, "Racist old biddy," then quickly burped and covered his comment with a big cough into his napkin.

"Jimmy," Mrs. Hillibrand said. "Enough."

I wasn't sure if she was chastising him for the comment or for his burp.

"No, it's okay. Your young man there may have a point. Edith lived to be pretty near a hundred, so she may well have had some old-fashioned notions. I wouldn't know for sure, since I barely remember meeting the woman," Gramps said. "But from what I hear, Edith never let anyone in—not even the mayor. Never took any invitations at all. A modern-day Miss Havisham she was, getting her groceries delivered to the front door and sending her laundry out."

"A Mrs. Who?" asked Jimmy. "Are you saying she wasn't an Eberlee?"

Mr. Hillibrand laughed. "No, son, don't you know your Dickens? Miss Havisham is one of the characters from *Great Expectations*."

"Oh, I read that in seventh grade," said Taylor. "She's the crazy old lady who sits around in her wedding dress. She was spooky and weird."

"Exactly. Miss Havisham was a crazy old coot," said Gramps. "I never heard anything about Edith being jilted at the altar, but"—he knocked on his head—"I don't think she was all there, if you know what I mean. Ask me, she had a few cobwebs in her closet."

"Angus T.!" Granny cried.

"Cuckoo, cuckoo," chirped Jimmy.

Gramps's teasing lightened the mood, which had felt heavy after Jimmy's comment about Aunt Edith not liking black people. Soon everyone had moved on to safer subjects. Granny asked Jimmy and Taylor what their favorite classes were. Jimmy answered lunch and Taylor answered gym. Mrs. Hillibrand asked Isaac and me the same question. My reply was a no-brainer.

"I like everything about school," I said.

"Yep, Miss Maebelle here is enrolled in the Gifted and Talented program."

"Oh," said Mrs. Hillibrand. "We have a smart cookie staying next door. Are you good at math, dear?"

"Yes, ma'am." I sat up straighter.

"Jimmy, maybe you want to hit Maebelle up for some help. Sixth-grade math isn't going to be at all easy."

"Oh, yeah," Taylor said. "Maybe you two can study down at Kiss-Me-Quick." Taylor held his linen napkin over his mouth, so I couldn't really see, but it sure looked like he was pursing his lips into a pucker.

"Knock it off, Taylor. There is no need to tease your brother," said Mr. Hillibrand, his deep voice booming.

Jimmy shot his dad a relieved look and then turned to his mom. "I don't need a tutor. I'm studying online."

Mrs. Hillibrand must've known Jimmy was embarrassed by those kissing noises, because she turned to Isaac. "And you? What's your best subject?"

"Oh, I like music. I play the trumpet. After school I have private lessons."

Mr. Hillibrand tossed his napkin onto his plate. "That's *you* we hear playing in the late afternoons and not Miles Davis?"

"Yep," Isaac answered, grinning to beat the band.

No one corrected Isaac, making him call Mr. Hillibrand sir. The conversation turned again, this time to jazz and blues greats. I stayed silent through it all.

"That was a fine meal," Granny said as she set down her fork. "We may never touch another slab of pork ribs."

"Hold your tongue, Ivory Ann! I'm never giving up ribs," said Gramps. "But that was a tasty supper. We thank you greatly for going to all the trouble."

"May I help clear?" I asked. I was itching to get to dessert, and the sooner we got dinner off the table, the sooner everyone would be oohing and aahing over my cobbler.

"Why, thank you." Mrs. Hillibrand pushed back her chair and I began collecting plates. Isaac hopped up to help too. He followed me into the kitchen and whispered, "What's wrong with you? Why didn't you come upstairs? Jimmy thinks you're snobby."

"Oh, really," I huffed. "And what do you think?"

Isaac shrugged and raised his eyebrows high. "You got me."

I hadn't gone upstairs because I hadn't been invited. Unlike Isaac, I didn't go where I wasn't wanted.

We put the first set of dishes on the counter and then both went back for more. This time as we swung back through the dining room door I said to Isaac, "FYI, tell Jimmy I don't care what he thinks. Boys are dumb."

And silly. While they waited for dessert, Jimmy and Taylor told each other bad knock-knock jokes like they were eleven and thirteen going on four. Why on earth did Ruth want a boyfriend?

Mrs. Hillibrand scraped the plates and loaded the dishwasher.

"Ma'am, thanks again for dinner." Isaac stressed the *ma'am* like I'd taught him. "I love Indian food. My mom did too. Her favorite restaurant was the Bapa Palace. She would have loved your cooking."

Mrs. Hillibrand busied herself putting on her oven mitts to snag the warming cobbler. She set it on the stovetop to cool. The kitchen smelled delectable.

"Oh, I love a woman who is a fan of good Indian food. It's my favorite. Is your mother coming to visit before the summer is up?" she asked.

She must not have heard Isaac clearly; here she was talking like his mama was going to pick him up in August.

"No, ma'am, she's not." Isaac bolted, saying as he went, "I'm going to see if we missed any plates."

Mrs. Hillibrand stared after him. "Did I say something?" she asked.

I chewed my bottom lip. "Um, Isaac's not blood kin, ma'am," I said. "My aunt lived in the same building and was friends with him and his mom. She adopted him about eight months ago, after his mom died."

"My word! I didn't mean to upset him." Mrs. Hillibrand got out the ice cream and bowls for cobbler à la mode.

"Can I ask you something?" I said.

"Of course you *may*," Mrs. Hillibrand answered, correcting my grammar.

I knew that rule. Something else was nagging at me. I was so flustered I'd made a mistake! "You asked Gramps what Edith was like, but with your living next door, you may have known her better than anyone. Why do you think she took the cookies y'all made but wouldn't welcome anyone inside?"

"I haven't a clue, but after the first two years of bringing her cookies, she baked us some in return—pecan sandies is what she made. The boys wouldn't eat them. Not a one. I had them cut the lawn and trim the hedges for her when the lawn service she hired didn't arrive on time, which wasn't very often, but it did happen. She was always very thankful." Mrs. Hillibrand smoothed her hands over her hair. "Now, I know the talk—that she was prejudiced, and she may well have been—but I got the feeling from time to time that Edith wanted us to be friends but didn't know how." Mrs. Hillibrand shook her head as if she was standing at Oak Alley's front door ringing the bell—and old Edith wouldn't answer. "Goodness me, let's serve this cobbler. It should be cool enough to dish out."

I stood nearby, hoping she'd ask me to help scoop cobbler or dish out the ice cream, but she didn't.

"Oh, no," she said. "First one faux pas and then another."

Little-Known Fact: Faux pas is French for "big, big mistake."

"First I hurt Isaac's feelings, and now I owe you an apology too."

"What? Why?" I asked, but then I saw for myself.

Mrs. Hillibrand tilted the bowl she had just filled with cobbler to show me. Instead of the scrum-delicious masterpiece the cobbler was supposed to be, all drippy and crumbly and good, it was dry and cracked. More like the desert than dessert.

"I must've forgotten to turn off the oven after the eggplant came out! Heavens! I am so sorry, honey." She dusted her hands on a kitchen towel. "Looks like it's just going to be ice cream tonight. How about I give you and Isaac an extra scoop to make up for everything?"

It was just a dumb cobbler, but right then it sure felt like the end of the world.

"Please, give my extra scoop to Isaac," I said, trying my best to keep my voice steady. "I got full on rice. I couldn't eat another thing."

· 22 ·

Little-Known Facts:
The human body is about 65
percent water.

The rainiest place in the world is
Mount Waialeale, Hawaii, which
averages 460 inches of water
a year.

If I were smarter, I could link those
facts somehow and make a word
problem. One for Jimmy Hillibrand
and his dessert-destroying mom to
solve.

I baked nonstop for the next few days. *Ugh.* I tasted my sixth blackberry cobbler disaster. This one was too tart. "No cobbler will ever be as good as that first cobbler. These berries aren't as good. Maybe Mrs. Hillibrand did it on purpose."

"Why would she do that?" Ruth asked, wiping the counter with a dishrag.

"I don't know. Maybe because her sons think Edith was a racist old biddy."

"Was she?"

I shrugged. "I never met the lady, how would I know?"

"But you're a mind reader."

"I don't talk to the dead, Ruth."

"Oh, okay, but what do you think . . . do you think she was racist?"

"Maybe," I said. "But I hope not. I mean, if it makes *me* feel icky to hear that, how would Isaac feel?"

I told her about the Oak Alley guest book, the locked wing, and the mini-fight I'd had with Isaac where he basically flat-out called my family slave owners. Ruth oohed and aahed in all the right places, and when I was done filling her in, she took a spoon and scooped out some of the cobbler I'd just made.

"This one isn't so bad." She put it in her mouth but she couldn't swallow it. She spit it into a napkin instead. She wiped her mouth and said, "Maybe it's not a blue-ribbon winner yet, but it's better than yesterday's. And the one the day before that. You'll get there."

"I stink!" I complained, dumping another fiasco in the garbage.

"No you don't—these berries do," Ruth said.

"Gee, thanks."

"Maybe it's the recipe." Ruth picked up the *Better Homes and Gardens Cookbook,* which I'd consulted after my third fiasco. Hannah V.'s ingredients were right on the money—all except for the lard, which I'd switched to shortening. Ruth flipped the pages.

"It's not the recipe. It's me and my talent for messing things up. If I don't watch it, my family is going to disown me."

The cookbook slammed shut. "What? Your granny and gramps love you."

"For now. But look at me." I glanced at my blackberry-splattered apron. "I can't do anything right and my parents get more and more famous every day."

"Really?" Ruth hopped around on both feet, like the Easter bunny at the mall. "Who's famous? Your mom? Your dad? Both? Are they in the movies? On TV? Tell me, tell me." Ruth continued to jump up and down.

"Stop jumping and I will."

Ruth stopped immediately.

I had opened this can of worms, so I reckoned I had no choice but to spill it.

"My parents were the relationship coaches on that TV show on the bus. The ones you thought were so in love."

"Oh, my gosh. You're a psychic and your parents are love gurus. My mother is going to flip! Why didn't you tell me? That is so cool."

"More like mortifying! All that talk about sharing and kissing and kissing and hugging."

"What?" Ruth asked. "I'm dying to be kissed." She looked at me all dreamy. "So what was it like? Kissing? Was it with mouths closed or open?"

I waved my hand in front of Ruth's face, trying to

break her boy-crazy spell. "Earth to Ruth, come in, Ruth. I never said I've been kissed. I haven't—not yet, and I am never kissing with my mouth open." I reckoned Ruth didn't know what *I* did about human mouths being dirtier than dogs'. And this didn't seem like the time to tell her.

"Oh, okay," Ruth said, sounding disappointed. As if she'd been hoping I'd tell her everything she needed to know about boys.

"*And,* it's not just my parents. My aunt Alice is this world-renowned doctor, and she's off lecturing in Switzerland—*and* Granny and Gramps are legends on the honky-tonk circuit." I paced the kitchen, from the counter to the table and back. "And Isaac—I can't forget Isaac—he's a trumpet prodigy!"

"Ooooh, wow," said Ruth, her mouth making the same shape as the long *ooooh* that came out of her mouth. "A prodigy, huh? That's cool."

"See! That's why I want to win a blue ribbon. I need something to show people I'm good enough. So I match the rest of my family."

Ruth whipped around the kitchen island and yanked me off the stool. Her fingers closed around my wrist and she led me over to the table.

"Ouch!" I said as she plunked me in the chair.

"Listen, I never want to hear that kind of talk again." She poked her finger so near my eyes I thought she might blind me. "That is what my mom says Oprah would call a defeatist attitude, and it is the kind of thinking that never, ever, ever leads to any good. You should know that! You're a psychic!"

"No, I'm not." I winced. There. The truth.

"You're not?"

"Nope, I'm not." I'd only known Ruth for a short time, but I'd liked letting her think I was good at something—that I was someone special. "The truth is I can't bake a cobbler, I can't play the trumpet, and I certainly cannot tell the future."

"Then why did you say you could?" Ruth sank into the chair opposite me.

"I don't know. You thought I was good at something without my even trying, and I didn't have the heart to tell you I wasn't." I played connect-the-dots in my head with Ruth's freckles, hoping the tears gathering in my eyes wouldn't fall.

"*Little-Known Fact: There are twelve different kinds of lies.* I can name them." Without even waiting to hear if she wanted to hear them or not, I started reciting: "Fabrication, a bald-faced lie, a lie by omission, a little white lie, a noble lie, an emergency lie, perjury, bluffing, misleading, a jocose lie—which is used in storytelling and joke-telling—a contextual lie—one that gives a false impression on purpose—and a promotional lie, which is a lie in advertising. I think there is a thirteenth, sugarcoating, but that could be classified as a little white lie. My psychic lie fits a lot of categories, but if we are splitting hairs, then *that*, I would say, was a lie of omission." I took a deep breath, trying to settle my stomach. "Mama and Daddy talk about those in their seminars. Married folks say those kind of lies a lot."

I reckoned Ruth wasn't impressed with my fact-finding.

She didn't say another word. I had finally stumbled onto what I was good at: losing friends.

"You know why I wanted you to be able to tell the future?" Ruth asked glumly.

"Why? To find out when you'd have your first kiss?"

Ruth shook her head. "I was going to ask you to look into your crystal ball or read tea leaves from your granny's teacup, or whatever it is that psychics do, and tell me if my parents are going to get back together."

Her face was blotchy. Spilling your guts could do that, I supposed.

"I like it here in Tweedle. I didn't think I would when my dad opened up his shop with an old buddy of his," she said. "I like hanging out with you and Isaac, but I miss my mom. And when I'm in Chattanooga with my mom, I miss my dad."

She fingered the cookbook's cover and brushed away some sticky flour paste.

"I wish I could help you there, but I can't." Ruth had spilled one of her secrets. It was time for me to spill one of mine. "I miss my parents too. At home, Mrs. Daniels, our neighbor, watches me when they're out late at parties or have to go away for weekends and can't take me. Sometimes I feel like they've divorced me. I've never told anyone that. No one."

After I told her that, she seemed even sadder. I wasn't doing a good job at getting her—or me—to feel better.

"You know what I don't get? Isaac's never sad. His mom died, he won't talk about his dad—and I never hear him complain. Ever."

Ruth and I glanced out the window to the backyard, where Granny, Gramps, and Isaac were practicing. Isaac sat there with the bell of his horn over his knee and his foot tapping away, ready for when his trumpet talent was needed.

"I didn't know all that. About Isaac," Ruth said.

"Yeah, he can be kind of a pest, but he doesn't have . . . what did you call it?"

"A defeatist attitude."

"Yeah, that." I sat there awhile, thinking. Isaac had a ton of stuff to be upset about. But he was the one who always had a smile on his face. He was the one who never complained. No wonder Granny and Gramps liked him better than me.

"You know what," I said, sitting up straight and doing my best to gather a second wind, "I'm gonna take a cue from Li'l Bit, as Granny calls him, and not give up."

"Awesome." Ruth hopped up. "I'll grab the blackberry bucket."

"Oh, I'm done with baking." I carried all the pots and pans to the sink and started washing. "But I am going to need your help."

Ruth wiped her hands on her powder-pink shorts. She bowed, like I had when I was pretending to be an all-knowing swami. "At your service, Maebelle T."

· 23 ·

Little-Known Fact:
Vincent van Gogh wasn't famous
during his lifetime. He only sold
one painting. He never knew
that the world would see him as
a great master.

If I don't win a blue ribbon, will
anyone ever think I'm great?

I decided to try reverse psychology. That night, after my
last cobbler disaster, I posted a sign with a skull and two
crisscrossed guitars to look like the crossbones on a pirate-
ship flag and taped it to the door of the locked wing,
where Gramps was sure to see it.

KEEP OUT
STAY OUT
That means you, Angus T. Eberlee, the new owner
of Oak Alley, who can do whatever he wants to with

whatever is behind this door. Have a garage sale, donate the clothes to Goodwill, or throw open the doors for all to see.

The next day, Ruth stopped to read the sign and chuckled.

"No defeatist attitude there," she said.

I couldn't give up on wanting to get into that locked wing. If it had been Josiah T.'s personal quarters, there might be a lot more than a silver tankard in there. Forget *Antiques Roadshow*—maybe I'd find something museum-worthy. Imagine that! Me, uncovering a family heirloom and getting to see it on display under glass. Maybe I'd even be asked to give a speech.

But I'd have to deal with the locked wing later. It was time to get my new blue-ribbon plan in action. I yanked open the front door. The day was *h-o-t*, hot.

Ruth plopped down in one of the wooden rockers. She'd been dressed regular in shorts and T-shirts, since that first day on the bus. "So what's the new plan? How can I help?"

I didn't get to answer. The Hillibrand boys suddenly came barreling down Oak Alley's dirt drive. They were racing, cutting one another off with their tricked-out bikes. They skidded to a stop by the front porch.

"Hey," Taylor said, a streak of dirt on his cheek. "Where's Isaac? We haven't seen him in a few days."

"Practicing. You don't get to be a prodigy without prac-ticing," I explained.

Jimmy jutted his chin. "Uh-uh. Being a prodigy

means you don't have to practice to be good. It comes naturally."

"So you're the expert on prodigies." I swatted away a mosquito.

"No, I asked my mom after your family came to dinner. All they could talk about was Isaac this and Isaac that."

"Oh, y'all are the Hillibrand boys. What a shame you didn't get to taste Maebelle's masterpiece." Ruth climbed out of the rocking chair.

"What masterpiece?" Jimmy asked.

"Her blackberry cobbler!" Ruth said, even though she hadn't tasted it either.

"It was the best one I ever made," I said shyly.

"How do you know?" Taylor asked. "My mom threw it away."

"That was her fault. Not Maebelle's," Ruth said, sticking up for me. "When it left here it was perfect, smelling sweet and tart and all a crisp and buttery brown."

I nodded. Besides being able to talk the ear off an alligator, Ruth was developing a good memory. She'd quoted me word for word.

"Who are you and what do you know about it?" Jimmy asked.

Ruth walked right up to Jimmy's bike. I bit the inside of my cheeks—as boy-crazy as Ruth was, I half expected her to plant one on him. Instead, she kicked his front tire. "Plenty! That was the cobbler to beat all cobblers."

Taylor held out his hands—the voice of reason. "Listen, no need to get hotheaded. What did you say your name was?"

"I didn't," Ruth said. She slammed her hands on her hips.

"This is Ruth. She's here for the summer like me, staying with her daddy. Ruth, this is Taylor Hillibrand and his younger brother, Jimmy." I made the introductions as nice and smiley as Mama would've, and then I added, "Ruth's my friend. *She* doesn't think I'm snobby, like some people do."

"If the shoe fits," Jimmy said. He twisted his hands on the handlebars of his dirt bike.

"Are you calling Maebelle snobby?"

"I sure am," said Jimmy. "But that's not as bad as what Isaac said about her."

I stood there gobsmacked.

"What? What did Isaac say?" I asked finally.

Jimmy talked slowly, as if what he had to say was so important it needed to be in slow motion. "'Maebelle thinks she's a know-it-all, but she's not. She's a know-nothing.'"

"I don't believe you," said Ruth. "Isaac would never say that."

"Believe it," said Jimmy. "C'mon, Taylor, let's go. I'll race you to the Kiss-Me-Quick."

"You're on." The Hillibrand boys pushed off, and at the end of the dirt drive where there was a paved curb Jimmy hopped it. I pinned my eyes to his back, wishing he had fallen.

"Forget about them," Ruth said, and then louder, "They're the ones who don't know nothing!"

"Anything," I corrected her. "*Any*thing."

· 24 ·

Little-Known Fact:
Dr. Martin Luther King, Jr., is the
only American to have a federal
holiday all to himself. The
presidents have to share a day.

Ask me, no one deserves it more
than Dr. King. He's my hero.

I spun myself around one of Oak Alley's fancy columns, thinking it would lift my spirits. All it did was make me dizzy. If I'd been in one of Mama and Daddy's Breathing and Being Boot Camps, they would have advised me to go talk to Isaac, to hear directly from him if what the Hillibrands had said was true. But Isaac and I weren't married. And there was no way I was asking him if it was true. It was.

Ruth grabbed my shoulders.

My body stopped spinning, but I felt all wobbly, like my legs had pins and needles.

"Listen, you are not a know-nothing, you are Maebelle T., soon to be a blue-ribbon winner."

"I am?"

Ruth nodded briskly. "Yep, so what's the deal? What ribbon are you going after now?"

I sat in one of the porch rockers and picked an ivy leaf off one of the nearby vines. "Here's the thing—you heard about the dance contest, right? What do you know about clogging?"

Ruth shrugged. "Not much."

"But I thought you took dance classes."

Ruth gave me a sideways glance, like Cotton did when he didn't understand what I was saying.

"Clogging is *the* dance of the South," I said.

"I know what clogging is, Miss Maebelle T. Encylopedia," Ruth said, putting her hands on her hips. "But I told you I took tumbling lessons. Not dance. And don't get all huffy with me when it's your cousin and those Hillibrand boys you're really mad at."

"Sorry." Old, old, old Aunt Edith's rosebushes were in the backyard. If they'd been up front, I would have picked an apology rose for Ruth. "I guess I can come across as kind of a know-it-all. I don't mean to be. I just like facts, is all."

"Well, I don't clog, and that is a fact," Ruth said. She shifted her weight to one hip. "Why are you so hung up on facts anyway?"

"Facts are set in stone," I said. "Once you know one, you know it forever. No one can take it away from you. Ever."

· 121 ·

"Well, it was a fact that my parents were married, and now it's not. Things change, don't they, even facts?"

I bit my lip. Ruth was right. Fact: I had once been in G & T and now I wasn't. Fact: I had once been Gramps's "one and only" and now I wasn't. Fact: Isaac's mother was gone and Ruth's parents were divorced. Circumstances were always changing. The only facts I could count on were the ones in my book.

Ruth sat in the rocker next to mine. "Listen, I can still help. I'm no clogger, but if you want I can show you how to do a mean backflip."

"Well, maybe you can throw one into my clogging routine. I've got a special favor to ask." I took a deep breath. "Will you be my choreographer?"

"Cory-o-grapher? What does that have to do with clogging?"

I grinned. "Everything! Call your dad and tell him we've going to the library while I let Granny and Gramps know where we're headed. Okay?"

"The library?" Ruth groaned. "Maebelle, we can't learn clogging from a book."

"Says who?"

· 25 ·

Little-Known Fact:
You can lead a cow up stairs but
not down them.

If I took a cow into Oak Alley,
could I talk it into ramming the
locked-wing door?

Ruth read all about the history of clogging while I scanned the shelves for a dance DVD. Maybe we could watch it in one of the AV rooms.

"Is there something I can help you with?" a distinguished-looking older man asked me. He had white hair and toffee-colored skin, and he was wearing a seersucker suit. "I'm Mr. Phelps, the librarian here. I haven't seen you among my charges before." He gestured to the shelves.

Charges? Who was this guy, Mary Poppins's long-lost brother?

"I'm staying with my grandparents, the Eberlees. I'm Maebelle T."

"Oh, you are living in Oak Alley." Mr. Phelps straightened his tie. "I have been meaning to get over there and say hello to your grandparents." He leaned in. "Have you been in the locked wing?"

I shook my head. Did the whole town want to know what was in there?

Granny hadn't given up searching for that key. Me either. Every time Gramps left the house we tackled another cabinet or searched through some drawer or another.

"No, sir," I said. "Why?"

"Oh, tarnation. I was hoping you had. I'm sure there are any number of treasures in there! Historical documents, maps, clothing, quilts!"

"I did find some recipes, though."

Mr. Phelps's eyes lit up. "You did?"

"Yeah, written by some lady named Hannah V."

"I'd love to see those recipes. I have run across the name Hannah V. before." He tugged on the cuffs of his seersucker jacket. "I'm writing a book on the history of Tweedle, Georgia. I've found a few things over the years to suggest that the Railroad might have run right through here before the Civil War."

"The railroad tracks by the bus depot have been here that long?"

Mr. Phelps's laugh was smooth as honey. "Not that railroad, Maebelle. The Underground Railroad. I have a feeling we had some abolitionists, folks who worked secretly against slavery, who lived in the area. I found some fake sale papers for several slaves, which tells me someone

· 124 ·

helped them escape, and I have been researching quilts found in the area for years. Are you familiar with the Underground Railroad?"

"Oh, yeah. We studied all that in school, stuff about safe houses, the drinking gourd, and Harriet Tubman, who was known as Moses because she led so many to freedom, and Frederick Douglass, who was a great orator."

He nodded. "I see you pay attention to your studies."

"Yep, you've got to keep up; otherwise you get left behind." I could see Ranjeet Malone and her big curls bouncing down the hallway away from me. "So you think there were abolitionists who lived out here in Tweedle way back when?"

"I think so, but I need more proof. That's why I am hoping to get to see inside Oak Alley. You see that quilt there?" Mr. Phelps pointed to a large colorful quilt that was encased in glass and hung up on the wall like a giant picture. "Slaves sewed quilts by hand, just as their mistresses did, but what their masters didn't know is that hidden messages were sewn right into the fabric—in the way that the blocks were laid out, or even in the way that the thread was sewn. On the backing of a quilt, knots were often tied in a grid pattern, two inches apart. These knots could mark distances between safe houses or other landmarks."

I moved in so close to the glass that my nose hit it and left a smudge mark. It looked like a regular old quilt to me. "So what does this quilt mean?"

"This one is in the tumbling box pattern. It isn't a true slave quilt but a replica. Quilts used to be hung on fences or porch railings to air out. Each stayed out for a period of time so that everyone who needed to on the plantation could see it." Mr. Phelps pointed to the quilt itself. "See the boxes cascading down? That signaled to the slaves that after months and months of preparation it truly was time to go. Have you seen anything like that lying around Oak Alley?"

I stepped back. "No, sir, I sure haven't. I've only seen flowery quilts, and ones with eyelet and lace, but I will keep my eyes peeled."

Wait until I tell Isaac! The town historian wanted into our house, Oak Alley, because he wanted to see if any abolitionists had lived there!

"Oh, I did find a guest ledger. It has some names in there from the 1850s! Maybe that will help. I can bring it by the library to show you, or better yet, you can come over and meet my granny. You can come for tea."

"I would like that." Mr. Phelps smiled. "I tell my patrons all the time, you never know what you are going to find in these here stacks—and today I found you, Miss Maebelle T. Helper. But I doubt you came here to help me with *my* research. It's my job to help you with yours. So what is it you are looking for?"

I'd been so wrapped up in the past, I'd totally forgotten about my future! My blue-ribbon-winning one!

"I'm looking for a DVD on clogging. You know, the dance, not a how-to on clogging drains."

"Oh, let's go over here to the do-it-yourself section." Mr. Phelps walked carefully, his gait slow and lopey like a giraffe's. We passed several brown metal shelves and he turned left and then right. "We'll skip the DVDs on plumbing and go straight to the ones on dancing." His long bony fingers danced across the shelf's contents until he found what he was looking for. "How's this?"

I took the DVD from him and read *Creative Clogging*. I tucked it under my arm. "Yep, this should work. Is there a room where my friend Ruth and I can watch it?"

"You can have AV room four for an hour. After that I need it as a changing room for when the Stroller Mamas arrive for story time."

"Thanks. And I appreciate the help." I didn't ask who or what a Stroller Mama was. I didn't rightly care. I'd gotten what I came for.

· 26 ·

Little-Known Fact:
Ruth was right! Facts change.
Pluto is now an ex-planet. It is
now "officially" known as 134340!
A number and not a name.

How sad for Pluto!

Turned out Ruth had met Mr. Phelps when she'd come to town over spring break. They caught up as he watched us slide in the DVD. Then he left us so we could get down to business. Ruth and I sat in green plastic chairs and watched the dance DVD three times. I was mesmerized. Knees, feet, legs, hands, all moved in unison, in groups as small as two and as big as twenty. The costumes ranged from big twirly square-dance-looking skirts to leather pants and blue jeans. The only thing the groups had in common was the kind of shoes they wore, all a soft-looking leather with taps on the bottom.

"Maebelle." Ruth sounded oddly far away, as if she

hadn't been sitting next to me gripping my hand as we watched. "I don't think clogging is for you."

"Why? It looks like fun. Hard, maybe, but fun." I pushed Pause on the DVD player. The dance group—they were called Dynamic Edition, and they even did some hip-hop moves in their clogging routine—all froze at once. They were doing some move where their arms were on the ground behind them and they scuttled on all fours like a spider, but in reverse. Their bellies were faceup, not down.

"You think you can do that?" Ruth pointed at the television screen.

"Sure can. Watch."

I plopped down on the beige carpet and stuck my hands behind my butt. I raised myself off the ground and scootched one way and then the other. I was pretty good, even if I did bang my head on the table.

Someone knocked on the door and a second later it opened. "What are you doing down there, Maebelle?" Mr. Phelps asked.

"Practicing," I said. "Ruth and I are going to put that move in our clogging routine."

"*Ours?*" Ruth stood. "You mean *yours*."

I hit Eject. "No, I mean ours. You saw for yourself. Clogging isn't a solo dance, so . . ."

"How exciting." Mr. Phelps checked his watch. "But your time is up. The Stroller Mamas are soon to descend, and honest, girls, I am not sure you should be here when they arrive. If there is anything they love, it is a girl who is of babysitting age." The door to the Tweedle branch library made a computerized *bing-bong*. "Too late, they're here. Don't say I didn't warn you."

A rush of women pushing strollers entered the library. A few carried babies in their arms or had toddlers slung on their hips. One mother made a beeline straight for the room we were in. "Clear out," she said. "Stoney has the runs, but he didn't want to miss story time. Not with all those wonderful voices you do, Mr. Phelps." She squeezed past Mr. Phelps and into the tiny room.

"I'll get the Diaper Genie, Martha. I was just clearing these two young ladies out of here. They are preparing a clogging routine—for the Anniversary Spectacular, I assume."

Before Ruth and I could gather our stuff, this Miss Martha woman had her sleepy son on the table and was busy yanking down his shorts. "So, you're cloggers, are you?"

"No, ma'am," Ruth said.

I elbowed Ruth. "She means not yet. We're both beginners, but we're quick studies. So I'm sure we'll pick it up lickety-split."

I wished I could plug my nose—the room was filling up with *s-t-i-n-k*, stink.

"Oh, well, there isn't much time left before the Anniversary Spectacular." The Stroller Mama went on. "If y'all want a viable routine before then, you should see my sister, Lucinda. She runs Diamond Dave's Dance Hall. Now, it's closed during the day, but Lucinda's there working on the books. You go down there, tell her I sent you, and she will whip you two into shape in a few weeks' time, give or take."

Miss Martha dug in her diaper bag, whipped out a clean disposable diaper, and had Stoney's old one off in no time. She whisked a wet-wipe out of a container and cleaned his bottom till it shone the same color pink as Ruth's shorts. She rolled the dirty diaper into a ball and sealed it by securing it with the tape tabs that had kept it on little Stoney in the first place.

The smell must've been getting to me, because I did the unthinkable: I stuck my hand out.

"I'll take that for you," I said.

"Well, aren't you a dear." Miss Martha handed over the diaper. She cleaned her hands on a wet-wipe and then she tweaked my nose. "I look forward to seeing y'all dance. I'll be in the audience, along with the rest of Tweedle— everyone is abuzz about the Eberlee Explosion! So if you need to find a friendly face, look for mine."

"Will do," I said. "Pleasure to meet you, and Stoney, too." I waved to the brown-haired little boy. He was still waking up from a nap, and his head lolled to the side like a rag doll's, but he curled his fingers at me and smiled.

I closed the door. I'd show those Hillibrand boys that I did know something. That when pushed, I knew how to play dirty.

"Why did you take that diaper?" Ruth asked in a nasally voice after I had closed the door. She had plugged her nose to keep out the poop stench. She sounded like she was underwater.

"I was just being polite," I said, smiling a sneaky smile.

I grabbed a plastic bag from the trash can in the hallway and wrapped the diaper up tight. Then I stuffed it in my book bag.

Ruth narrowed her eyes at me. "After your lesson on lying, I know when I've been fibbed to. What are you going to do to those Hillibrand boys?"

I hoisted my backpack over my shoulder and headed to the library checkout. Ruth had a library card, and a DVD player at her dad's. Maybe we could practice there. "That's for me to know and *them* to find out."

Little-Known Fact:
Every letter of the alphabet is used in this sentence: The quick brown fox jumps over the lazy dog.

I tried to come up with a sentence of my own that did the same thing, but I couldn't. *Know-nothing. Know-nothing. Know-nothing.*

Dinner was just about on the table when I got home—mac and cheese with sliced hot dogs baked right in, which was how Gramps knew I liked it, and a spinach salad. I only had time enough to toss my book bag in my room and wash up before grace was said—I didn't have time to think about the dirty diaper or how to use it to surprise-attack the Hillibrand boys.

I slid into my seat, next to Isaac and across from Granny. We bowed our heads. "We give thanks for the bounty of the food before us and for the God-given talent that lives inside us," said Granny.

"Amen," we all said. My stomach twisted. I sure hoped I was included in that prayer.

As soon as the prayer was over, shop talk started: there was no getting away from the Eberlee Explosion.

"You guys really have to let loose," Isaac said to Granny and Gramps.

Granny agreed, telling us how something called scatting—improvised mumbles and stuff that came from deep down inside, that expressed how moved by the music you were—was way harder than she'd thought.

"I learned something today too," I said, through a mouthful of mac and cheese.

Isaac kept jabbering away. "Oh, scatting isn't hard. You guys do it all the time in country singing. Just at the end of songs, not in the middle."

"*Y'all,*" I corrected Isaac. How many times did I have to tell him *y'all,* not *you guys*?

"Ooops." Isaac grinned at me. "*Y'all.*" He strung out the word so it sounded like *ya-owl.* "I keep forgetting that. Thanks, Maebelle."

I got ready to go for it again, and I barreled ahead like a freight train. "So you know that locked wing—"

This time they· heard me. "You aren't to go in there, Maebelle." Gramps took a swig of his iced tea and set it on the table with a thud.

"I didn't!" I defended myself.

"Good. Whatever is in there caused my family a bunch

of heartache—my dad used to curse this place under his breath. That's the only reason I knew Oak Alley existed."

I eyed Granny. She didn't do or say a thing but sat silently with her hands in her lap.

"But, Gramps." I set down my fork. "What if whatever made the family tree split was just some kind of misunderstanding?"

"Misunderstanding, misunderschmanding. It caused bad blood," growled Gramps. "I can't say we would have hung on to the place if your granny and I hadn't been talking about retiring."

"But what about its history? It's family history! You would've sold it to strangers?"

Gramps scowled at me and his eyes cut to Isaac. "All the history this family needs is sitting around this table right here, right now," he said. "Whatever happened between my dad, his father, and Edith doesn't matter a lick now."

"Fine," I said, knowing I shouldn't push it any further. "But I still think you should read that letter she wrote you."

"What letter?" asked Isaac.

"The one Aunt Edith wrote before she died—her lawyers gave it to Gramps," I explained.

Oops—me and my big mouth!

"Ivory Ann?" asked Gramps.

"Guilty as charged," Granny said. "And I know we aren't taking a vote on it, Angus—that letter is yours, and yours to do with it what you want—but I think Maebelle is right. You should open it."

"Don't open it." Isaac's voice wobbled.

"Really?" I leaned forward, plopping my elbows on the table. "What if your mom had left you a letter? Are you telling me you wouldn't read it?"

"Maebelle, that's enough," Granny said. "This isn't the time or the place."

"Fine." I crossed my arms over my chest.

We ate silently for a few moments, trying to shake the unease from the supper table. What had I done that was so wrong?

The longer we ate in silence, the worse I felt.

Isaac broke the tension. He held his fist to his lips and blew into it like his trumpet. Strange sounds, kind of like a harmonica and kind of like a bugle, filled the air. The notes went way low and then climbed back up. Eventually, Gramps picked up his spoon and grabbed Granny's from her place setting and began to thump them on his knee. *Rat-a-tattle-ta-ta-tattle. Ta-ta-rat-rat-rat.* Instead of singing, Granny took a gulp of her water, then leaned her head back and gargled, adding a bubbling percussion sound to the mix.

I didn't have a thing to add. Even my humming would be off-key.

I considered sending my plate soaring across the room. The crash would have been music to my ears, but that would have gotten me grounded for sure. And Granny and Gramps had never had call to put me on punishment before. They might even have phoned Mama and Daddy—and then I would've double gotten it. Grounded now and later.

I did my best to ignore the impromptu sounds of the

Eberlee Explosion and shoveled in forkful after forkful of my mac and cheese. I was so mad that I sucked in a deep breath as I was about to swallow. A hot dog chunk caught in my throat. I started choking. Not even coughing, just turning a terrible shade of crimson, I was sure.

"*Ugh-ugh,*" I gagged. The music stopped.

"Goodness!" Granny hopped up. "Raise your arms over your head, Butter Bean." She started thumping my back.

"No, no." Gramps grabbed a glass of water. "Here, drink this."

I felt light-headed. Was that how I was going to end up getting my picture in the paper, because of death by hot dog?

Isaac pulled me off the chair and hugged me from behind and pushed in my stomach up under my rib cage with his fists. It hurt, but it worked.

I sputtered, sounding like Winnie when her engine didn't want to turn over. "*Ble-ble-blech.*" That hot dog bit went flying into the spinach salad.

"Bull's-eye," said Isaac.

I gulped in a big breath. The Heimlich maneuver! I had done it on Ranjeet in the cafeteria last year, and the next day she'd given me a gift card and told the whole school I was a hero. "Heroine," I'd corrected her.

The room stopped spinning. I could breathe again.

"Thank heavens you're okay, Butter Bean," Granny said, hugging me tightly.

"You scared the devil outta me." Gramps lifted me under the arms and then wrapped me in his arms. It was perfect. The exact right amount of bone-crushing hugging accompanied by picking me up off the ground and swirling me in a circle.

"You scared me, Maebelle," Isaac said.

"She scared the dickens out of all of us." Gramps set me back down and thumped Isaac on the back. "Thank goodness, Isaac saved the day."

"That he did." Granny gave him a relieved smile. I knew it was on my account—that he was getting praise for saving me. It was like when G & T made a banner that said MAEBELLE T. (FOR FAST THINKER) EARL and hung it on the blackboard the morning after I'd saved Ranjeet.

"Thanks," I muttered to Isaac. "Fast thinking."

No one sat down again to eat—not with my hot dog loogie in the middle of the table.

"Looks like supper is done," said Gramps. "Ivory Ann, since I cooked tonight, you've got dish duty."

"That I do." Granny clapped her hands. "Isaac, you ready to help clear?"

Isaac looked at me with hopeful eyes. He hated doing the dishes by hand, even though all he had to do was scrape the plates and dry. Granny did the rest, or Gramps. They switched off every night, and Isaac and I every other, so we could get alone time with each of them.

"Nope," I said, "no get-out-of-dish-duty-free card for you."

· 28 ·

Little-Known Fact:
A *Wrinkle in Time* was turned
down more than two dozen times
before it got published.

Talk about t-r-y-i-n-g, trying hard.
Thanks for not giving up, Ms.
L'Engle.

Gramps blew Granny a kiss and he and I wandered off into the parlor. For a while, a long while, things were quiet. The music and then my choking fit had brought us all back together, but I was still angry. Why was Gramps being so stubborn about old Edith? It was one thing to leave the locked wing locked, but why not read that letter she'd left him? And Isaac? He had no right to tell Gramps what to do about that letter. Yes, he was part of the family, but that didn't give him voting rights. And we weren't even having a family meeting.

There was nothing I could do about any of that now, so I settled down to work.

The screen door was open and a nice evening breeze blew in. Gramps read the latest RV magazine and I got to cutting. Without modern technology, like a TV or a DVD player, or even a laptop, I'd have to make do with the old-fashioned learn-to-dance method: cutting out feet. Kind of like paper dolls, but not. First, I hauled out some art supplies from the bin Granny had made for Isaac and me for when we got tired of playing board games. Then I copied the outlines of my feet on page after page of green construction paper. That took *f-o-r-e-v-e-r*, forever. So to save time, I stacked a bunch of papers up and tried to cut through them with one swoop of the scissors.

"What're you doing, darling?" Gramps asked when he noticed me struggling.

I'd gotten the heel of the foot cut out, but after that it was no longer smooth sailing. The pile of paper got jammed between the scissor blades.

"Learning to clog. I have to cut out feet since we don't have a TV or DVD player. Ruth is going to do it with me. We both promised to practice tonight. Tomorrow we're going to meet with a real choreographer."

"Why don't you try cutting fewer pages?" Gramps kicked off his tennis shoes. He'd canceled Edith's garden service and spent the afternoon mowing the lawn, and little flecks of grass stuck to his socks.

"No, I can do it." I grunted as I squeezed. "I've just got to try harder."

"Does this dance routine mean Cotton won't be eating any more blackberry surprises?" Gramps liked to razz. But I didn't need reminding that Cotton was the only one around here who hadn't tired of eating my blackberry blech.

"Yep, I'm on to bigger and better things."

Gramps leaned over and patted me on the head. "You remind me of your mother. There wasn't one bit of quit in her when she was your age. Still isn't."

I stopped cutting. "What? Stuff didn't come easy to Mama?"

"Not a chance. She got where she is today because of hard work. Do you know how long it took to write that book and make those workshops they lead a success? Let alone end up on those big-time TV shows?"

I didn't have an answer for that. Mama made everything look so easy. I couldn't imagine her not excelling at something—*snap!*—like that.

"Took ten years, Maebelle. They've been at it since you were a year old. Your daddy wanted to pack it in a number of times, but my Melody wouldn't let him."

"Never thought of it that way," I said. Mama and Daddy had worked plenty hard to get to where they were. But I worked plenty hard too, and I seemed to be getting nowhere. I wanted to toss those papers with my dumb feet plastered all over them into the trash.

But I couldn't. Isaac and Granny were still in the kitchen cleaning. Plus, I wasn't a quitter. I wasn't!

"You know what would help, Gramps? Sing something for me?"

Gramps sat back and rubbed his flat belly. "What do you want to hear? Something from the Top Forty or an Angus T. original?"

"You pick," I said. "I'm all ears."

I kept cutting—or trying to cut—as Gramps leaned back in the armchair, waiting for the right song to hit him.

He started off slow and low, but then he picked up the tempo.

"I've got me a grandbaby, but now she's getting grown
Almost as tall as her mother—
Tell me, who would've known?
One day I used to rock her, set her up on my knee,
Play patty-cake and hide-'n'-seek
And watch silly cartoons on TV.
But those days are behind us now
And I don't know where they've gone,
Which is why I call this my 'Ode to Maebelle' song."

Though the song was silly, something in the back of my throat caught. Gramps was doing what he'd done when I was little. He used to sing to me and then tuck me in, whenever he could wrestle bedtime duty away from Mama, on their visits to our house.

"Got no idea where the time went,
Though I know we can't get it back.
That girl who used to play with jacks
Is now tall and strong, her noggin full of facts."

I laughed and set down the scissors and climbed onto Gramps's lap. I wished I was an itty-bitty thing again, so I could curl up and go to sleep there. He squeezed me and breathed in the smell of my hair; then he tapped his foot, and my whole body was rocking. I moved with him, swaying this way and that.

"The apple sure did fall far from the tree,
'Cause her Gramps has gotten his name on marquees,
But he is no G and T scholar like his dear, dear
granddaughter."

I didn't like him singing a lie. I opened my mouth to tell him the Truth with a capital *T* . . . but Gramps kept on singing. He dug deep and went for broke, tossing out his arms and knocking into one of the knickknacks. I caught it—an angel playing a harpsichord—and Gramps went right on singing. Granny and Isaac wandered in from the kitchen to catch his big finish.

"He is just a simple
Backwoods fisherman—
That's right, I'll sing it one more time—
He's just a simple
Backwoods knucklehead
Dumb-da-da-dummy!"

Gramps knocked his knuckles on his head. He beckoned to Isaac and he smooshed us in one of his bone-crushing bear hugs.

"But a very lucky, that's right, a darn lucky Grampy!"

And before I could give Gramps the proper thanks for *my* song, Isaac piped up, "That was awesome. Can you make one up for me?"

"Sure, I'll call it 'Ode to Isaac'!" And without even

having to take a moment to dream up a melody or anything, Gramps launched in, growling, and Granny joined
him, humming and slapping her thigh to the beat.

"I've got me a grandson, and the blues is in his blood.
Born in Chicagoland, but growing deep in the Georgia
mud.
He don't complain, he don't shake a stick,
Not my grandson, our boy is pretty slick,
'Cause life ain't been easy for Li'l Bit, not since the day he
was born,
But he has the power to blow his mighty horn.
Music and his mama gave him a strong will to live.
We're glad he is here with us—
That's right, we're glad he is here with us.
We weren't complete until he was here with us
'Cause the Eberlees and Earls have got a lot of love
to give."

· 29 ·

**Little-Known Fact:
June 6 is National Yo-Yo Day.**

I could teach Isaac to "walk the dog," but he's allergic.

I was as wrung out as Mama's hand-washables, with my heart twisted this way and then that. Gramps had sung, *"We weren't complete."* His song gave voice to what I had suspected all along: I wasn't enough.

I grabbed my cut-out feet off the floor. I had to get out of there, and quick.

"I'm going to my room," I said. "Ruth and I are meeting with a dance instructor tomorrow."

"Oh, sounds professional," said Granny.

"Yep, our clogging routine is going to be great. So I better get to it."

"Me too," said Isaac. "I'm almost done with the song I'm writing. I want to play it for you guys soon. Maybe play it at the Anniversary Spectacular."

"*Y'all!*" I shouted at him as he ran back into the kitchen, for goodness knows what. "It's not *you guys*, it's *y'all*."

"Oops. That's right." He came back with his trumpet case. It wasn't heavy, not like a tuba or anything, but it tipped him to the left. "I'm getting better at saying sir and ma'am, though."

"That you are," Granny said. "You two have fun up there."

I stomped up the stairs. Why couldn't Isaac stay in the parlor with Granny and Gramps? They wanted him—and I didn't. Not in the bedroom next to mine, connected by our shared bathroom.

"Hey, Maebelle, wait up. I want to show you something." Isaac trailed a step or two behind me.

"What? What is it?" We stopped outside my open door. My stinky backpack was directly behind it.

Isaac sniffed the air. "Did those hot dogs give you gas?"

"NO!" I slammed my door shut behind me. I kicked my backpack with the dirty diaper inside across the room.

"I didn't mean to embarrass you. It's okay if you tooted. It happens," he said through the closed door.

I opened the door a crack. Isaac sat on top of his trumpet case, waiting for me. I stuck my head out the door.

"Listen up, Li'l Bit. As the saying goes, whoever smelt it, dealt it." I shut my door again. "Go play your trumpet. I've got work to do."

· 30 ·

Little-Known Fact:
dit-dit-dit, dash-dash-dash,
dit-dit-dit

That's Morse code for SOS.

We ate earlier in Tweedle than Mama and Daddy did on their book tour. Mama'd given me a copy of their itinerary, listing where they would be and when. I checked the date. They had left New York, had been to Philadelphia, and currently were in Chicago, Isaac's hometown. Illinois is in the central time zone, an hour behind us, so I decided to call them anyway. I snuck down the hall to Gramps and Granny's room and dialed Mama and Daddy's cell. Mama answered on the third ring.

"What is it, honey? You sound like you've been crying," Mama said. I could tell she was walking out of a noisy room into a quieter one.

I snuffled up my snot. "No, I'm fine."

"I know when my baby girl is fine and when she's not. What's wrong?" Mama asked.

In the background I could hear the soft strains of music drifting through whatever fine restaurant they were in. There was a violin and a cello—maybe even an entire string quartet—but Mama's voice sounded so close it was like she was right there beside me, stroking my hair and letting me know everything would be A-OK.

"Oh, Gramps just sang a song and it made me a little sad," I said.

"Something they're playing at the Anniversary Spectacular?" she asked.

I had told her all about the spectacular on our other calls. I had made it sound like it was going to be the best day of my life, getting to sit in the audience and cheer on the Eberlee Explosion.

"No, this one he made up just for me."

"I love it when he makes up songs on the spot," Mama said. "They make you feel so loved."

"That they do. He sang one for Isaac, too."

"So tell me, how's Isaac? Is he adjusting to things?"

Isaac. He was the last thing I wanted to talk about.

"Okay, I guess. He's teaching Granny to scat, he agrees with Gramps on *everything*, and he never complains."

"Hmmm . . . Isaac must have some complaints. It can't be easy to be thrown into our family—the bunch of us oddballs." Slowly, Mama's therapist voice started creeping in. "Granny told me about the song he's working on about his mom. Have you heard it?" she asked.

"Yeah, but he's not done yet."

"Ah, well, maybe he's channeling his emotions into that. That's a good thing, especially if he's not talking about how he feels. You are practicing your active listening skills, aren't you?"

"I don't *really* have a choice. Isaac plays that trumpet morning, noon, and night."

Mama laughed like I'd said the funniest thing. But I *was* listening morning, noon, and night. Even now I could hear him down the hall, warming up with his scales. He was drowning out the sound of Mama's silky voice. "You are a card, Maebelle. Oh, here's your dad. He wants to say hello."

She passed the phone to Daddy and I went into Granny and Gramps's bathroom so I could hear him better. Before he could ask me about my day, I asked him about his. He told me all about their breakfast meeting, followed by a lunchtime book signing and then a baseball game at Wrigley Field, where he had picked up Chicago Cubs caps for Isaac and me.

"You can wear it next summer when you stay with Aunt Alice. You're going to love Chicago. The lake, Navy Pier . . . and they have the best corn dogs!"

"I don't have to go to Chicago for a corn dog, do I?" I asked.

"No, no, but the family put our heads together and decided that it would be good for you and Isaac to spend the summers together."

The family—as in all the adults—had decided without even talking to me?

"What about Granny and Gramps? I want to spend summers with them."

Daddy said, "Well, maybe they can go to Chicago too.

They've got the Field Museum and the Museum of Science and Industry. You'll love it, darling."

"I'm sure I will," I said. Isaac might have saved me from death by hot dog, but who was going to save me from a summer in Chicago?

· 31 ·

Little-Known Fact:
Trumpets have been around
since at least 1500 BC. A simple
one with no valves was found in
Egypt in Tutankhamen's tomb!

I bet *he* closed his music case
at night.

"Maebelle. Maebelle T!"

The sound of screaming woke me up. At first, I thought the house was on fire, and then I remembered: in the middle of the night, I'd done something bad. *Way* bad. I'd decided I wasn't going to be doomed to spend every summer with Isaac for the rest of my life. Not if I could help it. So I tiptoed through our shared bathroom, and in the dark I tossed that baby diaper I'd taken from the library into Isaac's room. I couldn't see well from the bathroom, but I aimed for his open hamper. I thought if I made a basket, Isaac might not find the source of the stink for a week!

"What? What's wrong?" I asked, walking into Isaac's

bedroom. "Ewww." I pinched my nose. "What smells in here?"

"Look!" He pointed at his trumpet case, which was on the dresser next to the hamper. The diaper had landed SPLAT on top of the horn's bell.

"Oh, no!" I hadn't meant for the diaper to land there.

Isaac pointed at his trumpet like it was a gigantic spider or some other movie monster. He started to cry, and not just a little bit, but like someone had kicked him where the sun didn't shine.

Jeepers. What had I done? My prank was anything but funny. It was *d-i-s-g-u-s-t-i-n-g*, disgusting.

"Calm down. It's okay. I'll clean this up." I grabbed a pair of dirty socks from the hamper and slid them over my hands. I grabbed the diaper. That Stroller Mama had called her son's poop the runs for a reason. Grayish green stuff dribbled out as I ran to the bathroom trash can. I tied the trash bag in a knot. I never wanted to see that diaper again. Ever.

I kept the socks on my hands and grabbed some antibacterial wet-wipes from the container on the counter. I went back to the open instrument case and scrubbed the sides of the trumpet.

My heart beat fast.

What I had done surely would get me out of having to go to Chicago, but not the way I wanted. Isaac would never talk to me again, which was fine, but neither would Granny and Gramps. Or Mama or Daddy. Or Aunt Alice!

I went back three more times for more wet-wipes. Finally, all the ick was off.

"See, all better." I peeled off the dirty socks and held his trumpet up to the morning light. It was clean and sparkly, as good as new. "See, nothing to cry about. Not a thing."

Isaac had squished himself into the corner with his back up against the wall. His knees were scrunched to his chest and he was so small he almost disappeared. "Why did you do that?"

"Me? You think it was me?" The words leapt out.

Isaac sucked up his snot. "Jeese, Maebelle, I wasn't blaming you."

"You weren't?" I sat on the edge of his bed.

"Where would you get a poopy diaper? Unless you trained Cotton to do a special animal trick for the Anniversary Spectacular." Isaac was drying his tears with the underside of his pajama shirt. "Or were hiding a baby in your room."

"Ha, ha," I said.

"What I was asking was why you cleaned it up," he said, his voice small and quiet.

I was about to tell him because I was a grade-A *j-e-r-k*, jerk, when we heard some ruckus outside.

"Go for it! Do another jump!"

The Hillibrand boys were outside doing bike tricks, the same as they had been yesterday. Their hoots and hollers got louder and louder.

Isaac sprang off the bed.

"I can't believe this." He paced the length of his room and back. "Jimmy and Taylor must've done it. They've got a baby sister, right?"

"Oh, yeah, Savannah." I didn't like the Hillibrand boys, but I couldn't let them take the fall for me. That would be as dirty as that diaper. "But why would they do that?"

Isaac sniffed again. "You got me. They asked me to go swimming a couple of times but I had to practice. Do you think that's why they did it? 'Cause I wouldn't hang out with them?"

"I'm not sure." How on earth was I going to get out of this?

Isaac tugged me by the arm over to his window. He showed me the trellis covered with ivy. "It had to be them! I was dumb enough to tell them that before the summer was out I wanted to jump from the trellis like I do from the fire escape at home. They totally could have climbed it."

"You think?"

"Totally! It was too cold in here with the AC on, so I slept with my window open last night." Isaac pointed to it. The dresser holding the trumpet case and the hamper were only a few feet away from the window. "It would've been easy." He leaned against his bedroom wall. The racing car posters he'd hung up looked out of place against the flowery wallpaper. "I just don't understand it, Maebelle. If they don't like me, all they had to do was tell me. Maybe I'm not as smart as you, but I'm not stupid."

Had he really just said what I thought he'd said? "You think I'm smart?"

"Duh, you know all those facts and everything. You're the smartest person I know."

"Really?" But what about his calling me a know-nothing to the Hillibrand boys?

"Yep, here or at home. Boy or girl—no one is smarter than you."

My heart swelled so big, I thought it might burst. Here I'd thought Isaac was hogging all the attention, but it sure sounded like Peanut Head looked up to me.

"But what about the hard time you gave me in the boat, telling me facts aren't good outside of tests?"

Isaac scratched his arm. "I'm not the world's best test-taker. I didn't want Gramps to think I was dumb."

"Please, how can a prodigy be dumb?" I asked.

"You sound like my mom. If I scored badly on some standardized test, she would tell me my mind was full of music." Isaac tapped his head. "But at least I'm street-smart—I can read people."

"Read people? Like reading a book?" I asked. "Read me."

Isaac squinched his nose like some kids did when figuring out a math problem. "Okay, but you may not like what I have to say."

"No, tell me."

Isaac did his best not to look hurt. "Well, I know you just put up with me because you have to."

"What are you talking about?" My heart beat fast. How did he know that?

"I heard Granny talking to you the night we first got here. She told you that you *had* to be nice to me, like it was an order or something. And then you wanted me to get lost at the swimming hole and didn't come upstairs to play video games at the Hillibrands'."

"What? I wasn't invited!"

"You still could've come. We're boys, Maebelle. We don't engrave invitations."

"Oh," I swallowed. That explained that. But what about Isaac calling me a know-nothing?

Isaac's face softened. He looked younger than usual. "I hoped here it would be different than back home."

"What do you mean? Tweedle is nothing like Chicago."

"Not the place. The people. After my mom died, the teachers made sure no one upset me—about anything. It was weird. No one teased me anymore. No one kicked me playing kickball. Everyone was too nice. That's why I like you—you're just you. You speak your mind even if it makes people mad."

"I do like you, Isaac, and not just because Granny told me to." Isaac was the straight talker, I realized, not me. That took courage. Deep down I wished I had more of that in me.

"Then why don't I get to hang out with you more? You're always slamming doors in my face and running off without me."

I shrugged. I'd never really thought about how that made Isaac feel, especially since it never seemed to bother him. "I like my privacy, is all. Plus, I'm just used to being Granny and Gramps's one and only."

Isaac shook his head. "I don't get that. I always wanted a brother or a sister, but my dad left me and my mom shortly after I was born. I never even knew him, saw a picture of him, or anything . . ."

I swallowed. No wonder he didn't want to talk about his father.

"... and then later my mom got sick. . . . I've been waiting my whole life *not* to be the one and only."

I did what I should have done all along. I opened my arms wide and gave Li'l Bit a big hug. "You know what, cuz? You're not alone. Not anymore."

· 32 ·

Little-Known Fact:
John Wayne, the greatest movie
cowboy who ever lived, was born
Marion Morrison.

No wonder he changed his name.
Maybe I should change mine,
too—to Maebelle T.-for-Terrible-
Cousin Earl.

Diamond Dave's Dance Hall was hard to miss. It was out past the center of Tweedle, where the speed limit went back up to fifty-five. Granny and Gramps insisted on dropping Ruth and me off instead of letting us ride bikes there. They were headed that way with Isaac anyway, on their way to a costume shop two towns over for the Eberlee Explosion outfits.

Gramps pulled Winnie into the lot, and she backfired, announcing our arrival.

Ruth piled out first. She stood in the parking lot staring, her jaw hanging open at the life-sized neon cowboy, who kept tipping his hat, day and night. I hopped down, my feet hitting the pavement.

Isaac moved to where we'd been sitting and buckled himself back in.

"What? You'd rather go costume shopping than watch us learn to clog?" I asked him.

"You mean you're inviting me?"

"I sure am." I felt bad about letting the Hillibrand boys take the blame for the dirty diaper, but I didn't know what else to do. Maybe this would make up for it—just a little bit. "Now, are you coming with us or what?"

"Go ahead," Granny said, winking at me. Gramps gave me one of his sly smiles.

I nodded in return and tipped an imaginary hat at the two of them—like that neon cowboy—before I raced Isaac to the honky-tonk's front door.

Little-Known Fact: Sometimes guilt makes you good.

• • •

As we strolled into the dance hall, Lucinda eyed us up and down. We didn't even have to say who we were. She left her paperwork and came right over to greet us. Granny had called that morning to be sure Lucinda really was up for teaching us a thing or two, and Lucinda had told her it was A-OK. "Ah, so, if it isn't Miss Maebelle T. and Miss Ruth. Are y'all ready for the toughest two weeks of your life?"

"Ma'am, yes, ma'am," I said, as if she were a drill in-structor and not a dance instructor.

"Good." She pointed one of her rhinestone-y finger-nails at Isaac, who had slunk into one of the booths. "And who is this here? My sister didn't tell me to create a dance for three kids, just two."

"Oh, this is my cousin, Isaac." I tossed my arm around his peanut shoulders. "He's just here to watch."

"Oh, no, he ain't." Lucinda clapped her hands five times in rapid succession. Like that, the jukebox began playing "The Devil Went Down to Georgia" and Lucinda started high-stepping it around the dance floor. Her back stayed straight, but her legs moved like lightning. She barely huffed as she yelled out over the fiddle, "If I am going to take time away from balancing the books to teach y'all, everyone, and I mean *everyone* in this here room is going to learn. You got that?"

"Yes, ma'am," Isaac said, sounding like a true-blue Southern boy. He ran from the booth and stood next to Ruth.

"You do want to win a blue ribbon, don't you?" Lucinda asked while her feet flew.

"Ma'am, yes, ma'am!" we hollered like new recruits.

"Good." She clogged it over to one of the booths and slid us a duffel bag, without once missing any of the intricate steps. "I used to teach at Kristy Lee's Clogging Academy—some of the spare shoes I've got in there should fit you. Tie those laces tight and let's get a-clogging! We've got some serious work to do."

· 33 ·

Little-Known Fact:
Clogging is as old as the hills.
Mountain folk, Cherokee Indians,
and Russians all did it.

Now it's my turn.

I couldn't believe my luck—I was actually a pretty good clogger! Or as Lucinda said to me all afternoon, "Not half bad, kid, not half bad." But if any of us was a natural, it was Isaac.

He could lift his knees up to his chest lickety-split. I didn't understand how he could get them so high, but when he and I were catching our breath on the sidelines while Lucinda showed a combination over and over to Ruth, he let me in on his little secret: "The kids at my school take the stairs two at a time, but I'm too short for that, so I just do them really quick so I don't get trampled."

Lucinda clapped her hands. "Isaac, come here and show Ruth the clog over vine with me."

"Happy to," Isaac said. And he bowed to Ruth as if he were at a ball.

I leaned against the booth, panting heavier than Cotton did after chasing a squirrel. I smiled to myself. Where Isaac lived everything had stairs: schools, apartment buildings, stores, train stations. All the schools down here in Georgia were as flat as a pancake, the same as the ranch house I lived in, but Oak Alley had stairs. At least eighteen in a row, two sets of nine on each staircase. As soon as we got back I was going to practice doing them double-time.

We took it from the top again. Dolly Parton's "9 to 5" blared from the dance hall speakers. It was a live version. The audience clapped and cheered as she sang. I took my spot between Isaac and Ruth and pretended that applause was for us three. I was kind of glad I'd been so bad at baking those cobblers, because dancing as a team sure was more fun than baking solo.

We worked our tails off learning the steps. Once we had them, after seven full run-throughs, we were done for the day.

I wiped my forehead with a handkerchief, sweating to beat the band.

"Good job today, y'all," Lucinda said. "Take the shoes with you, and take these CDs I made and these step notation sheets and practice at home. I've got a stock order coming in tomorrow, so I'll see the three of you back here day after next, got it?"

Ruth was so exhausted she nodded at me to get her stuff.

Isaac grabbed the other step sheet. "There's only two," he said to Lucinda.

"I was only expecting the two girls." Lucinda gulped some water. "All my sister told me was to be especially nice to Maebelle since she took one of Stoney's dirty diapers off her hands."

Was that the reason Lucinda had told me I wasn't half bad—because she was supposed to be extra nice to me? Then, as if my ears had been plugged with water, and had suddenly unstopped I heard, really heard, what had been said. Lucinda had mentioned the diaper. The DIAPER!

"Oh, Maebelle, did you get those Hillibrand boys good?" Ruth hopped up and down, her energy returning.

There was no denying it now. It was plain as day: the diaper ending up on Isaac's trumpet was no one's fault but mine.

I turned to him. "It was me," I said. "Not the Hillibrand boys."

Just then, through the open dance hall windows, we heard Winnie's horn, announcing Granny and Gramps's arrival.

Go on ahead and kick up those heels!
Cut yourself loose and see how it feels!
Pick your team right, 'cause it's Saturday night.
Welcome to the hoedown showdown!

Winnie's horn stopped, but none of us moved toward the exit. If only Granny or Gramps had honked before the word *diaper* had spilled out of Lucinda's mouth.

"Maebelle, what did you do?" Ruth wrinkled her nose, probably remembering that gross diaper. This was worse than admitting I wasn't a psychic. Way worse.

Isaac shoved the CD and papers into my hands. "She smeared that diaper on my trumpet and then let me blame it on the Hillibrand boys."

"Maebelle!" Ruth screamed. "You didn't."

"I did."

I hung my head. I didn't bother telling them that I hadn't smeared it. That what I had intended to do wasn't nearly as bad as what I had done. It wouldn't matter a bit. What I had done couldn't be defended. Isaac had every right to be mad.

Isaac stalked away and Ruth crossed her arms and shook her head. "Maebelle T. Earl, you are blue-ribbon bad."

"I know," I said sadly.

· 34 ·

Little-Known Fact:
Je suis désolé means "I am
sorry" in French.

Isaac looked at me bug-eyed
when I said that to him.

If the ride home in Winnie was strained, Granny and
Gramps didn't notice. Granny jabbered on about the costumes. Black jeans and yellow T-shirts with black se-
quined vests. It sounded to me like the Eberlee Explosion
was going to look like bumblebees. And Gramps sere-
naded us with the lyrics to a new song he'd written on the
back of a Hardee's bag when he and Granny had stopped
for lunch.

Isaac sat in one of the middle seats and Ruth and I
took the couch in the way back. She elbowed me a couple
of times, whispering, "I can't believe you, Maebelle T.-is-
for-Temper," but that was all that was uttered about the
dirty diaper incident. I reckoned the only reason Isaac
didn't tattle on me was because he knew I was sitting in a

big old bowl of guilty-as-sin stew. We dropped Ruth at her dad's shop—Cletus's Car Repair—and after a stop at the farmstand, where Granny bought some corn on the cob, we headed back to Azalea Avenue. A mile and a half later, we were home.

"My, my," said Gramps as Winnie bounced along the dirt drive. "Looks like we've got a visitor. Are you expecting anyone, Ivory Ann?"

"No, not me," Granny answered. I snuck a peek out the window. It was Mr. Phelps. He was wearing a yellow seersucker suit instead of the blue one he had had on when I met him. I waved but I didn't think he saw me. He was sitting in one of the rockers and using his hat as a fan, since it was hotter than Hades outside.

Gramps shut off the ignition and Isaac jumped out of Winnie, lickety-split. He ran down the walkway and straight for our guest—my guest.

"Hi, are you lost? The Hillibrands live next door, if you're looking for them."

"Pleased to meet you, son—oh, and I know where the Hillibrands live. I've been to their place many times. I'm here to see Maebelle."

"You are?" Isaac's frown asked its own question: *Why is he here to see you?*

I stepped onto the shaded porch and resisted sticking my hands on my hips.

"Mr. Phelps, this is my gramps Angus T., and my granny Ivory Ann, and you met my cousin Isaac. Mr. Phelps is the town librarian." I stood back while the triangle of handshakes and hellos crisscrossed one another.

"We've been out all afternoon, so now isn't really a good time for tea."

Mr. Phelps threw back his head and laughed. "I wouldn't show up unannounced for that. I came by to ask you a favor."

"You did?" I puffed out my chest.

"I did. I was wondering if you would be my research assistant. I am hunting down the true identity of someone referred to as Ruby Red. I am getting pretty caught up in reading some primary sources I dug up, and I'd love to have your help copying and logging the materials I've already assembled. There are twenty-five boxes of Turner House papers among those from the Macaulay estate."

"Turner House? Is that where General Turner lived?" I asked.

"Yes, but he wasn't a general then. The war hadn't started yet. The fire that burned down his home was in the summer of 1859, or so my records say.

"So how about it? Would you like to pitch in?"

"When I'm not at clogging practice, I'd love to help. Is that my official title, research assistant?"

"It can be. I'll make you up a name tag and everything."

"Cool!"

Mr. Phelps bent over and dug around in the soft leather briefcase he had with him. "In case your answer was yes, I brought you some reading material. This should ground you in the subject matter." Mr. Phelps handed me a book: *Hidden in Plain View: A Secret Story of Quilts and the Underground Railroad.*

"Awesome."

There was a quilt draped from an old brick window on the cover. After a quick glance I pressed the book to my chest. I hadn't told anyone what Mr. Phelps had said about Oak Alley maybe being a stop on the Underground Railroad, and I didn't want them to find out now.

"Are you sure you can't stay for a nice cold glass of lemonade?" Granny fanned herself with a swatch of fabric from the costume store. The sequins caught the sun and sent streams of light every which way, like a disco ball. It made me dizzy. I went to put a hand on Isaac's arm, but he pulled away. I plopped down in one of the rocking chairs instead.

"No, no, I do need to be going. I am just on a short break from the library. I need to be back in time to lead story hour. The Stroller Mamas never miss a one." Mr. Phelps turned to me. "You haven't been inundated with babysitting requests, have you, Maebelle?"

"No, sir." I gulped.

"Good. 'Cause when word got out how you offered to help Mrs. Fairbank with Stoney's diaper the other day, I would have thought each of those kind ladies would be calling you and begging for your services."

"Oh, Maebelle, your mother would be proud of you. Emptying all the garbage and taking it to the bins this morning, without anyone asking, and helping this lady at the library. That was awfully kind of you," Granny said. She patted me on the shoulder.

"Sure was," Isaac growled. Now he knew how I had covered my tracks and disposed of the diaper for *g-o-o-d*, good. "*Awfully* nice."

"Well, it was a pleasure to meet y'all," Mr. Phelps said, "and especially you." He shook Gramps's hand. "Edith kept to herself, that's for sure, but she did keep an eye on your career. Whenever the Rootin' Tootin' Bootin' Band came out with a new recording, she put a hold on it and had me run it over and place it on the porch. If you ever consider opening the locked wing, please let me know."

Gramps, who had been smiling the whole time Mr. Phelps was speaking, now asked briskly, "Why are you interested in that wing?"

"Oh, pardon me, I thought Maebelle would have told you—"

"The book he's writing is all about the town," I interrupted. "From back when it began one hundred and seventy-five years ago." Gramps had had his chance to learn that one of his relatives may have been an abolitionist.

Mr. Phelps chuckled. "That's right, you see—"

"History is a total mystery," I said. "Ha! That rhymed."

Isaac rolled his eyes.

"Yes, well, Maebelle has quite the noggin. She will be an asset, I am sure." Gramps's tone let me know he was glad I was helping Mr. Phelps, but I was *not* to set one foot in the locked wing—as if I could. I still hadn't found the key, and Granny's recent searches had turned up nothing but lint and a couple of mothballs.

"Well, I've got to be going. Hope you enjoy that book, Maebelle."

"I'll start it tonight," I said. "I can't wait."

Granny added, "And do come over one day for tea.

I'll make some biscuits and we can have strawberry short-
cake with fresh whipped cream."

"A delight!" Mr. Phelps said as he sauntered off, his
gait as slow as when he walked the library aisles.

Everyone else went inside to cool off, but I stayed on
the porch and opened the paperback book Mr. Phelps had
brought me. If history was a mystery, I aimed to solve it.
At least, when it came to Oak Alley, I did.

· 35 ·

Little-Known Fact:
Mr. Phelps must think I'm smart.

That book he gave me is
h-a-r-d, hard.

I was wondering why Mr. Phelps had given the book to
me, since most of it was way over my head and not a bit
of it had to do with anyone named Ruby Red, when I
came across a Post-it stuck on a double-page spread.

It said: *Maebelle T.—take a good look at the quilt code. Let
me know if you spot anything that looks like these around Oak
Alley.*

I had no idea what the quilt code was, but the entire
book explained it, and on the pages Mr. Phelps had
marked was a chart that showed what symbols sewn into
quilts meant. The code was told to the author by an old
woman named Ozella McDaniel Williams, who sold
sweetgrass baskets in a big market in Charleston, South
Carolina.

Ozella had told the lady to write it down, and she did.

It was kind of like a riddle. The slaves wouldn't necessarily act after each quilt was shown. They would memorize the signals, signs, and directives for when the time came to flee to freedom.

This was what I read that night.

Monkey Wrench

The monkey wrench turns the wagon wheel.
This meant to stay on the alert.

Wagon Wheel

This one meant to pack up—like packing a wagon. Also not to take too much, only the essentials.

Bear's Paw

The wagon wheel turns toward the bear's paw.

That Ozella lady said this pattern was really about following animal tracks, which would help slaves find water and keep them headed north to freedom.

Crossroads

The bear's paw led to the crossroads.

The crossroads meant Cleveland, Ohio. Lots of historians (maybe even ones like Mr. Phelps) said Cleveland was a major stop on the Underground Railroad. Many escape routes led from there to Canada.

That was enough for one night. There was a lot more to the quilt code, but my brain was all zigzaggy trying to understand. Everything Ozella had told the author was common knowledge to slaves. It wasn't common knowledge to me. I was glad to see it written down and even gladder Mr. Phelps had chosen to share it with me. Now I knew what to look for, even if Ruby Red still remained a mystery.

· 36 ·

Little-Known Fact:
Astronaut Neil Armstrong left
some mementos on the moon,
including a small gold pin shaped
like an olive branch, the symbol
of peace.

I know where to find blackberry
bushes, but where can I find an
olive branch?

That night, well after midnight, I woke up for the umpteenth time. My bedtime quilt-code reading had entered my dreams. I kept seeing bare feet running in the woods, slapping the dirt and hitting the water as dogs barked in the distance. I rolled over in a panic and when I jolted awake, I heard a bark I knew: Cotton's. He must have seen a squirrel.

I was just drifting off again when Isaac slid into my room without knocking. He was carrying a flashlight. The bright beam of light swept across my room.

"Maebelle, wake up."

"I'm awake, sort of. I was having a hard time sleeping." I sat up, the light almost blinding me. "Can you please get that out of my eyes?"

"Sorry," he said. He sat on the corner of my bed. "No, no, I'm not sorry. You're the one who should be sorry."

"I am sorry, Isaac. I never meant to hit your trumpet. Honest. Please, tell me how I can make it up to you." I'd march right into Granny and Gramps's bedroom and confess if that was what it took. "I'll do anything. Take all your turns doing dish duty, play Marco Polo at the swimming hole when we're not clogging, let you beat me at Chinese checkers. Anything!"

Isaac crossed his arms over his chest. "All I want is to know why you did it in the first place."

I played with a string on my pajama top. I wound it around my pointer finger until it hurt. "Didn't you ever do something without thinking—something that once you did it, you didn't want to think about it?"

"What are you talking about?" His voice was small in the dark. He pointed the flashlight at the comforter, and only a little spot of light leaked out.

"Throw someone's homework away? Take money from your mom's purse? Not tell your best friend something LIFE-changing?"

"You did all those things?" Isaac's voice shot sky-high. "You didn't steal from Granny and Gramps, did you?"

"No, no, I didn't do any of that, except the last one." I

scooted under the covers and listened to the soft hiss of the air conditioner push cool air through the vents in the floor. "Can I tell you a secret?"

Isaac didn't answer. I reckoned he didn't much care what I had to say, but I went ahead and told him anyway.

"I'm not in G and T anymore. I've been too embarrassed to tell Granny and Gramps."

After I said it, I wondered if I had answered his question—part of it, anyway. I had been feeling bad when I got here—feeling like I didn't belong—and then when Isaac had showed up, that not-good-enough feeling had turned into flat-out feeling replaced.

"Is that why you've been so moody? Nice one day and mean the next?" Isaac asked.

"I guess. And I know what I did was mean and rotten and terrible, but I wasn't aiming for your trumpet. I was trying to make a basket in the hamper. That doesn't make it any better," I went on, not even stopping to take a gulp of air. My voice cracked. "And I am really, truly sorry and I understand if you can't forgive me and will hate me forever."

"Maebelle, hush!" Isaac shoved me gently. "I'm mad—for sure—but no one hates you. Don't be so cinematic."

"That's what Granny calls me."

"I know."

Isaac lay down next to me. He didn't get under the covers but stayed on top. He turned the flashlight toward the ceiling and drew figure eights with the beam. Neither of us said anything, but with each figure eight he made I could tell he was less and less angry. Something was softening inside him—the same something that was softening inside me.

He set the flashlight faceup on the nightstand and flipped over onto his stomach. "You aren't the only one around here with a secret on their mind. I've got one too," he said.

I remembered what Mama had asked me—if I was being an active listener. I reckoned she hadn't been talking about listening to Isaac's trumpet-playing.

"You want to talk about it?"

Telling Isaac I was no longer in G & T didn't feel good, but it didn't exactly feel bad, either. The only word that came to mind was *clean*. Telling the truth made me feel clean.

"No." He shrugged, as if what he had on his mind was no big deal, but I could tell that it was. "No one knows, not even Alice."

"Really? You keep secrets from her?" I asked.

"Yep, everyone has secrets. My mom did. She had one—a doozy is what Gramps would call it."

I couldn't imagine what kind of secret Isaac's mom had had. "Well, I've always got an ear to listen if you want to talk."

In the soft glow from the flashlight I could see him grin.

"You know, I thought about stealing one of Savannah's diapers next door, or following Cotton around with a pooper scooper and getting you back."

"You did?"

"Yep, I was going to plop some poop in your *Little-Known Facts* book."

"You wouldn't," I said.

Isaac laughed and crawled out of bed. "That's for me to know and you to find out."

I could tell Isaac was teasing me, but it made me feel better—like maybe I wasn't the only one around here capable of a grade-A mistake. I plumped my pillow as Isaac padded over to the bathroom door. Before closing it, he said, "Hey—you meant what you said about doing anything to make up for that dirty diaper deal, right?"

I gulped, wondering what I was in for. "Yeah."

"Good. Two things. One: Clogging is cool, but I don't want to be the only boy dancer. I'm going to ask Jimmy and Taylor to join our clogging team, and if they say yes you've got to be nice to them no matter what."

Yikes! But I agreed quickly. There was no way he was going to talk the Crash 'Em and Dash 'Em–playing Hillibrand boys into clogging.

"And two: I get to be a research assistant too. What was that book Mr. Phelps gave you about?"

"It's about quilts and how messages were sewn into them," I said, revealing as little as possible for now.

"Really? What does that have to do with Ruby Red?"

"You got me," I said.

"I guess we can find out together," Isaac said. "Don't forget to be like a dolphin and sleep with one eye open."

"Ha, ha." I tossed my pillow at him, but he was too quick. It bounced off the bathroom door.

37

Little-Known Fact:
Long before there were quill
pens, ancient men and women
wrote with hollow straws or reeds
filled with berry juice.

How cool—another reason to love
the blackberry!

When I climbed out of bed, it was almost noon. Isaac
was gone, Granny and Gramps with him. There
was a note on the counter next to a stack of pancakes.

Butter Bean,
    Tried to wake you but you were sound asleep.
Must've been all that dancing you did yesterday.
Anyways, we're off to Savannah on some errands.
Gramps needs some new strings for his guitar and
Isaac wants a new mouthpiece for his trumpet. Poor

kid, when he jumped from one of those oak trees out in the yard his horn landed in a pile of Cotton poop. (Reminder: use the plastic bags under the kitchen sink to pick up any doodoo you see in the front or back.)

We should be home by 5 p.m. We left you some pancakes. You can eat them cold with some strawberry jam. There are sandwich makings in the fridge for lunch, and we will bring home some grub for dinner—maybe chicken fingers and Texas toast—so you have something to look forward to.

Stick close to home. Mrs. Hillibrand is going to check in on you today, but if you need anything head on over there. We'll be back before you know it.

Love you bunches,
Granny and Gramps

P.S.: Guess what? Jimmy and Taylor said YES! Clogging with five will be better than three, I promise. And if you read more of that book Mr. Phelps gave you, I want to hear all about it.

Later, gator!
Isaac

I folded the note. A part of me wondered if they really had tried to wake me, or if Isaac had just wanted to get

Granny and Gramps away from the house to tattle on me. Maybe the note they had really wanted to write went something like this:

Dear Maebelle,
    Not only are you no longer our one and only, you are no longer an Eberlee-Earl. Isaac told us what you did—tossing that diaper on his trumpet— and given your actions, we can no longer call you family. We can't stand to be around you. So we left. We hereby bequeath Oak Alley to you, and know that you will live in spinsterhood—a shut-in for the rest of your life, following in old Edith's footsteps—as punishment for your crime.
                No longer your loving grandparents,
                Angus T. and Ivory Ann

P.S.: Granny and Gramps are coming with me to Chicago. We're going to play the jazz joints there. Sorry we couldn't stay, but you are too hideous to be around.
                So glad we're not blood family.
                Isaac

I shook my head. I was being silly. Isaac wasn't mean and vindictive—like I was, or had been. After our talk last night I felt better. "Forward momentum" was what Mama and Daddy's relationship book would call it.

I grabbed a pancake and headed outside to check on Cotton.

"Just you and me, boy." I stuck the pancake in my mouth and untied his leash from the tree. He bounded to me, but I stood up before he could get my pancake all slobbery from one of his kisses. "This is *my* breakfast—go eat your own."

Cotton waddled over to a clump of tall trees. Gramps or Granny must've filled his food and water bowls before they left. Or maybe even Isaac. I'd seen him petting Cotton sometimes, rubbing his snout or his belly. Isaac always washed up in the kitchen sink or even with the backyard hose before heading up to his room. Maybe we were all getting to like one another. I could tell Mama the next time she called we really were a true-blue family—dog and all.

I climbed the porch stairs and sat in the same spot Isaac had that first day I had heard him play his trumpet. I leaned back and let the sun warm me the same way Gramps had when we'd been taking a breather out on the fishing boat. I ate my pancake slower than slow, savoring the chunks of bananas and walnuts that Granny had loaded in there. Somewhere in the middle of my chomping and chewing and breathing and swallowing, I jumped up.

I called out to Cotton. "We've got the whole house to ourselves! C'mon, boy, inside. Now!"

Somehow, some way, I was getting into that locked wing—today.

38

Little-Known Fact:
Muhammad Ali was born Cassius
Clay. Most people know that, but
what they don't know is he was
named after his father, who was
named after a white fella,
Cassius Clay, a Southern
landowner and abolitionist.

How about that?

Since I was the only Eberlee-Earl home today, I was going to make my own rules. Rule #1 was that Cotton was allowed in the house. I'd clean—mop, sweep, and vacuum—wherever he went so Isaac wouldn't have some strange allergy attack and think I was out to get him. Rule #2 was like the one for swimming: never go exploring by yourself. I called Ruth, hoping against hope that she'd come over.

"Isaac is my friend too," Ruth said. "What you did was wrong."

"It was. I'll understand if you never want to see me again. Isaac has to, since we share a bathroom and all. Maybe that's why we're friends again."

"Isaac forgave you?" Ruth asked. "Why didn't you say so? I'm not a psychic either, you know. I'll be there as soon as I can."

"Thanks, Ruth. Bye."

I hung up the phone, feeling less alone. Until Ruth arrived, I'd have Cotton by my side.

"You ready to go hunting, Cotton?" I scratched the spot behind one of his droopy ears, a move he liked so much his tail wagged double-time. "Nope, it's not rabbits we're gunning for but a key. If you see anything shiny, you let me know."

Cotton followed me into the dining room. We went straight to the hutch where Granny had showed me Josiah T.'s tankard. If that had made its way out of his private quarters, maybe other items had too. One by one I took every item out of the hutch and placed it gingerly on the dining room table. I found some china, linen napkins, and a chest lined with maroon velvet that had a bunch of silverware and serving spoons inside. There was one little utensil that looked like a teeny tiny pitchfork.

"Look at this, Cotton. What do you think this was used for? Eating a sprig of spearmint?"

Cotton barked, trying to grab at the little fork as if it were food. When he did, he knocked over a little container of silver-plated toothpicks. They rolled onto the floor, as thin as regular wooden toothpicks but unbreakable.

A toothpick. Maybe I could use it to pick a lock!

I leaned down and rubbed Cotton right between the ears. "You are a lifesaver, Cotton, a true-blue lifesaver!"

I replaced all the silver toothpicks but one and headed off for the locked wing.

. . .

Every so often, I tucked a wisp of hair behind my ears. Jiggling with the latch was hard work, and I had no idea if I was doing it right. I hadn't ever run across any B and E—breaking and entering—tips in my *Little-Known Facts* book. I kept at it, though. Cotton never once left my side.

After what felt like forever I glanced at my watch, sure I had been concentrating on jimmying the old-timey door lock for at least an hour or more.

It had been fifteen minutes.

"*Boo-roo-roo,*" Cotton barked.

"Shhh, boy, I'm not giving up. I'm not." I had my ear to the door and it sounded like that silver toothpick might have made contact with something.

"I think we're almost . . ." *Click.* "In! Oh my gosh, Cotton, we're in! We're in! We're in!"

I turned the door handle. Whatever secrets my B and E crimes would reveal, there was no turning back now.

· 39 ·

Little-Known Fact:
Charles Lindbergh was the first
pilot to fly solo nonstop across
the Atlantic Ocean.

There is something to be said for
taking chances.

"It's now or never," I said. My heart beat quickly, as if at any moment Granny, Gramps, and Isaac would somehow surprise me. Even if they arrived home early and didn't honk, Winnie might backfire. Either way, I'd have plenty enough warning to skedaddle before they caught me.

I stood in the doorway shaking. After all this time, I was scared to go into the locked wing alone. Ruth better get here quick!

"Here we go, Cotton. Off into the unknown."

Cotton trotted beside me as I crept down the hall, feeling like Harriet from *Harriet the Spy*. Only differences were I wasn't wearing eyeglasses and it was way too hot to wear a sweatshirt like the kind Harriet wore on the book's cover.

Halfway down the hall I stopped. I was coughing from all the dust, and I didn't think I could go much farther. I pulled my T-shirt up over my mouth to keep the dust from gagging me. I chanced it, pressing on. Dusty sheets were tossed over everything, and when I peeked under them I caught glimpses of paintings, side tables, antique oil lamps, iron sculptures. None of the ladylike stuff—porcelain bells and such—that was sprinkled through the rest of the house.

Every painting I uncovered was of the house or the lake, not a portrait. Ever since Giles had mentioned that the Kiss-Me-Quick Bridge was named after Josiah T., I had wanted to get a glimpse of the kissing bandit myself.

Cotton and I searched each room: some room that smelled of stinky old cigars and had a marble-looking chess set on a fancy corner table, a study with books galore, a private dressing room where trousers and topcoats still were stored in mothball-ridden trunks, and a gun room that had muskets and silver swords mounted on the wall. I still had no clue what Josiah's job had been or why he needed a private wing.

"I don't get it, Cotton. Why is this wing locked? I'm not finding anything that would cause a fued between Gramps's dad and his sister. What gives?"

Cotton *boo-roo-roo*ed his response. He was just as confused as I was, I reckoned.

"We might as well keep searching." I nodded at the last closed door at the very end of the hall. It was the one I had tried to peer into from the yard.

The wooden floor creaked as Cotton and I made our way in. The window faced the side yard, which was all open space and walnut trees. Heavy drapes hung there, as they did in all the other windows. I tugged them open so I could see the room better. Sunlight streaked in. There was a mirror so old it had brown tarnish spots where there should have been a reflection. I pulled off a sheet and uncovered a huge four-poster bed, hand-carved—maybe from one of the oak trees on the property.

We were in Josiah T.'s bedroom! What was it doing down here and not upstairs with all the others?

I held my breath as the dust storm subsided. Cotton slumped at my feet—the heat must've been getting to him—but we couldn't turn back now. There was a quilt on the bed. It had yellowed with age, from not being washed since forever, but it had large stars and small stars sprinkled all over the fabric. The stars rose up puffy in some areas and lay flat in others. I hadn't seen anything like it in the quilt code. Was it something to help the Southern slaves find their way to freedom? Was Mr. Phelps right— had abolitionists lived here?

I proudly fingered the fabric; it was soft and cool despite the heat and mustiness of the room, but it had just as much dust covering it as everything else did. Yuck. My hand was coated thick. I tried wiping it off on the edge of the bedside table, but I ended up knocking into a pile of books. They fell on the floor. Blue leather-bound books, a red one, and one, a black ledger, not much different than the Oak Alley guest book I had found in the entryway.

I picked that one up. In faded gold lettering were the words: PROPERTY OF JOSIAH T. EBERLEE.

I held the ledger to my chest. It wasn't as good as seeing a picture of the man himself, but it was close. I hugged it hard, feeling the connection from me to Gramps, and Gramps to his dad, and his dad to his dad, and back as far as it took to get to Josiah T. Eberlee, the Kiss-Me-Quick ladies' man.

I opened the ledger; there were columns on each page. It was an olden-day spreadsheet. The first part of the book tallied the crops: Corn. Green Beans. Tomatoes. Cotton. How much had gone to market and how much had been used here at Oak Alley. The second part of the book tallied livestock: Cows. Sheep. Pigs. How many had been sold and how many gone to slaughter to put food on the table.

I turned the page to see what other animals Josiah and his family—my family—had owned. But on that next page, still under the livestock section, in the same tight but readable script, were names. First names only, followed by initials:

Thom C.
Lucretia C.
Phillip K.
James T.
Tanner S.

Sophie T.
Vendetta V.
Hannah V.

And after the initial there was a date and a dollar amount, from $150 to $500.

The book fell straight out of my hands with a thud. A cloud of dust sprang up in my face as Cotton bolted from beside me and took off down the hall back to the main part of the house. I wanted to follow him, to get out of there, to pretend I had never come back here, but I couldn't. I couldn't move or breathe.

The ledger that lay spread on the floor told an ugly truth.

Josiah T., the Kiss-Me-Quick ladies' man, had been no abolitionist. He had been a slave owner.

· 40 ·

**Little-Known Fact:
Daniel Boone rarely wore a
coonskin cap.**

How much of history is true and
how much is false?

The doorbell rang. Luckily, Gramps hadn't yet found the time to get the doorbell rigged to play the chorus of "Hoedown Showdown," which he was always teasing Granny that he was going to do. It rang again—*ding-dong-ding, ding-dong-ding.*

It was only when I heard Ruth shout my name that I unfroze.

"Coming! Hold on," I yelled. "I'm in the toilet."

I pronounced it *twa-let,* hoping Ruth would remember Grace, the wrinkly bus driver who'd driven us here to Tweedle, and would remain my friend forever—no matter what.

I barreled out of Josiah's room and quickly shut the door to the west wing. I didn't have time to relock it. I could get back in if I needed to—not that I ever wanted to set foot back there ever again.

"'Bout time you got here," I said as I yanked open the heavy front door. "You're never going to believe—"

"Hi, Maebelle, what took you so long?" Ruth asked, cutting me off before I said a word more.

She stood between the Hillibrand boys and in front of Mrs. Hillibrand, who stood behind them all like she had gathered a flock of lost sheep.

"Yes, dear, we were getting worried," said Mrs. Hillibrand.

"Yeah, we thought you'd fallen in." Jimmy elbowed Ruth, but she didn't laugh.

"I was coming up the drive as the Hillibrands were walking over to check on you," Ruth said, trying to explain why they were with her.

"Oh, yeah." I lingered in the open door.

I didn't want to ask them in, but if I didn't it would be r-u-d-e, rude. Especially after the way old Edith always kept everyone waiting on the front porch. "Come on in."

"So is everything okay, dear?" Mrs. Hillibrand asked as she stepped into the foyer, followed by her two boys. Her eyes swept the grand split staircase and the crystal chandelier that hung above it. "You looked in quite the panic when you opened the door. Is it because I caught you red-handed?" Mrs. Hillibrand asked, with a twinkle in her tone.

I gulped. She had. There was no use denying it.

Gramps was going to kill me. The first time he and Granny had left me alone at Oak Alley and I had disobeyed them. I didn't know which would be worse: having to admit to them that I'd broken their rules or having to tell Gramps that he—like me—was the direct descendant of a man who had sold *people*!

Mrs. Hillibrand tapped her fingernails on her arm impatiently. "I'm sure your grandmother has the same rule I do: no friends over when the adults aren't home. And here we find Ruth, who the boys introduced me to, bounding up the drive. What was it y'all were intending to do?"

My scared-stiff heart started beating again. Mrs. Hillibrand had caught me, but she hadn't *caught* me.

"Oh, Ruth was coming over to rehearse our clogging routine for the Anniversary Spectacular," I explained, thinking on my feet. That wasn't why I had invited Ruth over, but it was only a small fib. "We were going to practice out back—on the porch, not inside, so really we're not breaking any rules. Isn't that right, Ruth?"

Mrs. Hillibrand raised a commanding eyebrow at Ruth. "Is that right?"

"Yes, ma'am, it is."

"It's a good thing you brought Jimmy and Taylor over with you." I motioned to where they were huddling together, craning their necks to try to see as much of the house as they could. "Isaac told me they're dancing with us. We can have our first big rehearsal today."

"Boys, how exciting!" Mrs. Hillibrand said. "I used to clog, you know."

"What can I say, Mom," Jimmy said. "Anything to make you happy."

"That's right," Taylor said, winking at his younger brother. "Anything for the ladies."

I grimaced. Taylor was always teasing Jimmy about being some kind of lady-killer. Mrs. Hillibrand laughed, though. When she stopped chuckling, she asked the boys, "So *really*, why are you clogging?"

"There's football tryouts at the end of the summer. Isaac told me the fast footwork in clogging will help me make the team. Give me a leg up, is how he put it," Taylor said.

Isaac *was* good at reading people. He had totally known what to say to make Taylor say yes.

Taylor continued, "And li'l bro here has other plans."

But neither Jimmy nor Taylor said what they were.

"All right," Mrs. Hillibrand said, heading for the front door. "Boys, I'll grab some lemonade and snacks and be back with a few pointers. I was quite the clogger in my day, I will have you know."

Mrs. Hillibrand closed the front door, and I waited until I could no longer hear her flip-floppy sandals hitting the porch stairs before I let out a sigh of relief.

"That was close," Ruth said, plopping down on one of the stairs. "I was worried you had gotten into the locked wing."

"The locked wing?" Jimmy said. "Are you serious? You got into the locked wing? Every kid in town wants in there."

Jimmy lunged toward the door. It wasn't hard to figure out which one it was—all the other doors on the ground floor were open, and the one I had just come out of was slightly ajar.

Cotton got all excited as I tried to block Jimmy. He began barking up a storm, circling my legs, and accidentally banged into the unlocked door. In my rush, I must not have gotten it shut too tightly.

The door swung open.

The hardwood floor was littered with my footprints and Cotton's paw prints in the inches-thick dust. Faded sheets lay in heaps here and there. There was no denying I had been in there. Cotton, too.

Jimmy, Taylor, and Ruth all crowded the doorframe.

"Whoa, every Halloween, kids talk about getting in through one of the windows, but no one has ever had the guts to do it for real. Totally spooky! More than the lame haunted house at school," said Taylor. He looked at me fully for the first time, as if I was the only non-chicken in town. "Find any dead bodies in there?"

Jimmy stepped inside. "Or any buried treasure?"

"Um . . . Josiah T. Eberlee wasn't a pirate." I rolled my eyes. "Believe me, there is no treasure, buried or otherwise. No dead bodies, either, but it is spooky. Dust and cobwebs."

"How long has it been locked?" Taylor asked. "We've lived here ten years, and the older kids used to tell us Miss Edith kept her cauldron in there."

"You got me. It could've been locked for twenty, thirty . . . sheesh, maybe even fifty or more years. Gramps came to visit when he was a baby, maybe it got locked around then," I said. "But no cauldrons or witches' hats. I'd rather have found one of those than what I did find."

Ruth stood on her tiptoes and swung her arm around

my shoulders. "Maybe my mom is the psychic. She said that something life-changing was going to happen here this summer. Did you discover a life-changing kind of thing?" Ruth asked.

I thought about how I had felt when I saw the slave ledger—like nothing would ever be the same. "I sure did," I said.

Little-Known Fact:
Some recipe collectors refer to
themselves as receptarists.

Maybe Hannah V. was one.

After that, I couldn't even hear myself think. Jimmy, Taylor, and Ruth all bombarded me with questions. I raised my hand and stopped them cold.

"I'll do better than tell y'all what I found, I'll show you. But first we've got to close the drapes and put those sheets back over everything before their mom"—I nodded to Jimmy and Taylor—"comes back."

There were a couple of grumbles about how hot and dusty it was, but with three times as many hands, the sheets were off the floor and back on the paintings and furniture in no time. I closed the draperies in Josiah's room. I'd closed the others as I searched since I didn't want anyone walking by the front of the house to see in. Good thing Josiah's bedroom faced the side yard, or Mrs. Hillibrand would've found me out for sure.

At first I avoided Josiah T.'s ledger, stepping over it where it had landed on the floor, but then, taking a deep breath, I snatched it up.

"Everybody out."

I made sure I still had the silver toothpick I'd shoved in my front pocket and I locked the door again so no adult soul—especially not Granny and Gramps—would be the wiser.

"Follow me." I stuck Josiah's ledger in my backpack and we all tromped through the kitchen to the screened-in and shaded porch. Everyone took a seat around the picnic table except for me. I stood at the head, like I was calling a meeting to order.

"I'm trusting y'all here," I said, eying everyone, "to keep what I am about to show you a secret."

"Even from Isaac?" Ruth asked.

"No, not from him. He's one of us," I said.

"One of us who?" asked Taylor.

I thought about it for a moment. Our dance team did need a name, and after the top-secret day I'd just spent, I had the perfect one. "If there aren't any objections, I hereby dub us five the Clandestine Cloggers."

"Can-des-what?" asked Jimmy.

"Clandestine. It's a big word for 'secret,' or 'meeting in secret,'" Taylor said.

"How'd you know that?" I asked.

He turned to me. "It was a vocab word. You're not the only ace student around here, you know." He half stood and ruffled my hair like I was his kid sister.

I smiled shyly, glad the Hillibrand boys didn't feel like

enemies anymore, but then I realized what I had to do. What I had promised to do.

"None of you might want to dance with me, in secret or not, when I show you what is in here." I tapped my book bag.

"Spill it," said Jimmy. "Show us what you've got."

I plopped my bag on the table and dug out my discovery. I stroked the leather cover, wondering where to begin. I reckoned it all started with Hannah V., who I had thought was family.

"I found some recipe cards stuck in a kitchen drawer written by a woman who I thought was a long-lost relation."

"That's where Maebelle got the blackberry cobbler recipe," Ruth said. "It has to be over one hundred years old."

"No wonder it tasted blechy," Jimmy said.

"You never even tasted it. No one did," said Ruth. "Not that first one."

I ignored Jimmy—he was trying to get my goat. The only one who seemed able to get *his* was Taylor, with all that teasing about girls and kissing.

"I also found an Oak Alley guest ledger in the foyer—you know, like the kind they have at weddings. It dated back to the 1850s and kept track of folks who came for overnight stays, you know, like sleepovers, and which family member they came to visit."

I was rambling. I set the ledger in the middle of the table.

"And then Mr. Phelps told me he thinks there were abolitionists who helped slaves escape right here in town, and that maybe a few of them even lived here at Oak Alley, so I totally knew I had to get in the locked wing to find out for sure. But I never expected to find this."

I opened the ledger to the last page I had looked at and pointed. Their eyes followed my finger.

No one said a word as they read.

"What's the biggie?" asked Jimmy. "Our family was farmers too."

"Yeah," said Taylor. "Our mom traced our family back five generations and then that was that. All she found were dead ends."

"Keep reading. You didn't get far enough," I said. Cotton came and plopped down on my feet, as if he could tell I needed consoling.

Suddenly, Taylor's shoulders tensed, and then Jimmy's. They must've gotten to the list of names. First names only—no last, just initials and price tags.

Ruth read it too. "You mean Hannah V. was . . ." She gasped and muttered, "Bless my heart," something I was sure she had heard her TV-talk-show-watching mama say in times of crisis. But it was as good a saying as any, and one that summed up exactly how I felt.

• • •

By the time Mrs. Hillibrand returned, I had repacked the ledger, shoving it in my backpack before I ran to help her through the fence gate. Her hands were full. She was carrying a large tray holding four jumbo thermoses full of lemonade, and a bunch of overstuffed plastic bags of chocolate chip cookies.

"They're soft and gooey," she said. "Homemade. Like the kind I made for Edith. I've been meaning to bring some over since I ruined your cobbler, Maebelle."

"Thanks," I said. I grabbed one of the bags and my backpack. "I'll run this stuff inside. Be right back."

I tossed the cookies onto the counter and ran to my room. I dumped out my backpack and hid Josiah's ledger between my mattress and boxspring. Then I grabbed my donated dance shoes and headed outside as quickly as I could.

When I got back, Ruth was showing Mrs. Hillibrand the step sheets Lucinda had given us, and the Hillibrand boys were hooking portable speakers up to an iPod.

"Do we really have to dance to 'Nine to Five'? That song is lame," said Jimmy.

"It's the song Lucinda picked out," Mrs. Hillibrand said. "I am sure the judges will like it.

"Girls, why don't you show us what you've got?"

The last thing I wanted to do was dance, but Mrs. Hillibrand didn't give us a choice. She cued the music and Dolly Parton's live rendition pounded out of the speakers. We had no choice but to attempt the steps Lucinda had showed us.

"Where are your dance shoes, Ruth?" Mrs. Hillibrand asked as we hoofed it. "Do you need me to get you some when I buy the boys theirs?"

"No, ma'am," said Ruth, staring down at her tennis shoes. "I've got some, just forgot 'em."

Mrs. Hillibrand was kind enough not to press the issue, and after about half the song was over and we got stuck, Mrs. Hillibrand did the steps with us. She carried Lucinda's step sheet, reading from it as we went. She was a good clogger. She kept her back straight and her legs moved in perfect time.

"C'mere, boys, let's work you in. I don't think Lucinda will mind. It's her step combos I'll have you doing."

The boys did as they were told. Taylor and I were the same height, so we got paired up in the back. Ruth and Isaac were the two shortest, so Ruth took the front by herself for now. Jimmy got to stand in the center, since he was medium height.

When Isaac joined us, we'd form a perfect star pattern. Just like the thick cotton quilt on Josiah T.'s bed—which looked nothing like any of the quilts I had read about in the quilt code book. It gave me a nagging feeling. Did Josiah's quilt mean something?

· 42 ·

Little-Known Fact:
The state motto of Texas is one
word: *Friendship.*

If it wasn't my motto when I
arrived in Tweedle, it is now.

Cotton lay at my feet while I rocked in one of the porch rockers, thinking how much could change in such a short time. The bunch of us had spent the entire afternoon clogging, and then when it got too hot we were invited to go swimming in the Hillibrands' pool. No wonder we hadn't seen the boys when we went down to the swimming hole—they had their own watering hole in their fenced-in backyard.

I had lent Ruth a swimsuit. We didn't play Marco Polo or anything. We lay around on inner tubes and pool noodles and talked about my Josiah T. discovery. Jimmy thought Josiah's having been a slave owner did make old Aunt Edith some kind of hater, but Taylor said that though Edith was odd, she had never done anything hateful, other than not let anyone inside. I kept waiting for one of them to call me a name—a mean name—since it was my relatives we were talking about, but no one did.

A few days earlier I'd thought the Hillibrands were bullies, but they weren't. They were just regular kids like me. I laughed thinking about how Ruth had kicked Jimmy's bike tire, defending me, and how even now, despite what I'd shared with them about Josiah T., none of them told me to get lost, to skedaddle and never show my face again.

I hoped the same would go for Isaac.

• • •

I snuck back into the locked wing with Granny and Gramps's rarely used digital camera and took a couple of shots of Josiah T.'s bedspread.

It was suppertime, and families all over town would be sitting down to their nightly meal. When Winnie pulled into the drive, I'd just put the camera away, and I ran outside to meet them, with Cotton trailing behind me.

"There's our sleepyhead," Granny said as she climbed out of the Winnebago. She kissed the top of my head. "Grab one of those bags in back. We got chicken fingers, just like we said we would."

"Yum." I could smell the fried chicken and honey mustard dipping sauce as soon as they opened Winnie's door.

"We hear you had a fun day," Gramps said.

"You did?"

How had he heard?

"We rang the house but got voice mail, so we called next door. Mrs. Hillibrand told us you were out back with the boys and Ruth."

"Yeah, we went swimming. Isaac, did you know they've got a pool?"

"Yep, I could see it from their bonus room upstairs," Isaac said.

I felt a slight pang that Isaac had known before me, but that didn't matter. What mattered was that we were all getting along.

"We practiced our clogging routine too. We're getting good. You were right, it's more fun to dance in a big group," I said, and then as Gramps and Granny carted in a heavy-looking speaker box, I told Isaac on the sly, "And I got into the locked wing."

"You *what*?" Isaac's voice jumped a pitch like a note in one of his trumpet solos.

"Shhh." I made sure Granny and Gramps were too far away to hear me. "I'll show you what I found later. We've got to take it to Mr. Phelps."

. . .

It wasn't hard to convince Gramps and Granny to let us ride their bikes downtown. The library stayed open until seven-thirty. All we had to do was promise to pick up a pint of Cherries Jubilee, Gramps's favorite ice cream, at the five-and-dime on the way home.

We slid the bikes into the bike rack and made our way inside. The place was empty. I plopped my book bag on the circulation desk and rang the little bell. "Mr. Phelps, you here? I don't know who Ruby Red is, but I know who he isn't."

"I am always here. I practically live here." Mr. Phelps sauntered out of one of the AV rooms. "Ah, if it isn't my research assistant."

"Why is Ruby Red so important?" Isaac asked.

"Ruby Red was an abolitionist. His or her true identity is what I need help finding out," Mr. Phelps said.

"I thought you said we were researching quilts." Isaac glared at me.

"We are," I told Isaac. "I hope you don't mind Isaac helping, Mr. Phelps. He wants to pitch in."

"The more the merrier," Mr. Phelps said. "But this is serious business."

"We know. The rest of the Clandestine Cloggers— Jimmy, Taylor, and Ruth—will be coming soon. We've all got a stake in what you're trying to uncover."

"We do?" Isaac raised his brow. "I don't care who Ruby Red is."

"You will." I nodded and pulled out the black leather ledger. "This isn't the Oak Alley guest ledger I told you about. It belonged to Josiah T. Eberlee. I found it in one of the rooms in the locked wing."

"Oh, I want to see!" Isaac reached for it.

But I gave it to Mr. Phelps, I needed him to look at it first. He took a seat at the circulation desk and thumbed through the crinkly-paged ledger. "Oh, this is a *find*," he said as he read along. Isaac tugged a stool next to him and read as best he could over Mr. Phelps's shoulder.

"My, Maebelle, you do have a nose for historical

research." Mr. Phelps slid open a drawer and got out a magnifying glass. "Did you know this relation of yours, Josiah T., was the best man at General Turner's wedding? Well, before he was a general."

"I knew they were friends." I told Isaac and Mr. Phelps about the tankard Granny found and what the inscription said.

Isaac folded his arms over his peanut chest. "No fair! You've been holding out on me. Granny has too!"

I patted his back. "Don't feel bad. I reckon she just wanted it to be our special thing."

How had I not figured that out before? As much time as Isaac got solo with Granny and Gramps, they still did things just for me, like getting chicken fingers and driving Ruth and me to dance lessons.

"Well, I'm glad you're telling me now," Isaac said. "What else do you know that I don't?"

Mr. Phelps answered that one.

"Well, we know that a few years before the war, Turner House burned down—the barn went first and then the fire spread. The house was rebuilt, but with the war preparations going on, it never was as grand again. In some of the correspondence I've read, it said Charles Turner never spoke the name of Josiah T. after the fire and never spoke to any of the Eberlees again. Good thing the Turner line died out years ago or we might have a real town feud on our hands."

I liked this Josiah T. fella less and less. "Do you think he started the fire? Josiah T., I mean."

"Don't know," said Mr. Phelps.

"I think he did," I said, full of conviction.

"Why would you think that?" Mr. Phelps asked.

"He was a rotten man. The worst." My chest tightened, and I pushed through the shame to the undeniable truth. "Just so you know, no one at Oak Alley worked to free slaves. They were slave owners. They even sold them off for money."

"Are you sure?" asked Mr. Phelps.

Saying it out loud was worse the second time around. "I'm sure."

"Can I see?" Isaac asked.

I took the ledger from Mr. Phelps and handed it to Isaac. He walked with the heavy book into the corner of the children's section. I went to follow him, but Mr. Phelps told me to hang back. To give Isaac some space.

Isaac flopped into one of the beanbag chairs and read aloud the long list of names I had already committed to memory:

> *"Thom C.*
> *Lucretia C.*
> *Phillip K.*
> *James T.*
> *Tanner S.*
> *Sophie T.*
> *Vendetta V.*
> *Hannah V."*

In the quiet of the library, it felt like Isaac's reading was a memorial. I flopped onto the big beanbag chair beside him.

"Are you okay?" I rubbed Isaac's arm. It was cold in the library and his arm hairs stood straight up. "It's awful, isn't it?"

Isaac nodded, his big eyes droopy, like Cotton's.

"Do you hate me?" I asked. I could feel blotches crawling up my cheeks. I felt on fire from the inside out.

Isaac had a look on his face I couldn't quite read. "Why would I hate you?"

"My family—they . . . Josiah—he—was terrible, a terrible man, and I acted terrible to you. Maybe being terrible and hateful is in my genes."

"But you weren't mean to me because I'm black, were you?" Isaac asked.

"No, no, I don't think so," I answered honestly.

"Then why were you?" he asked.

Isaac deserved an answer—a real answer. "I've been thinking about that. Everything was changing, and when my parents told me I had to spend next summer in Chicago, I was scared. I wanted things back the way they used to be. Back when I was the one and only around here."

Isaac punched my arm. "Well, that was dumb. You are the one and only around here. The one and only Maebelle, don't you know that?"

"That's right," said Ruth.

I didn't know when Taylor, Jimmy, and Ruth had arrived, but they had. They sat on the carpeted steps that ringed the area where the Stroller Mamas sat during story hour. Before I knew it, we were all talking about how seeing that ledger had affected us.

"It's weird. My mom talked to us about how most likely we're the descendants of slaves," Taylor said. "But it took looking at that ledger to get it. Really get it."

"To get what?" I asked.

"That slavery didn't just happen in the movies," said Jimmy. "Or in books, you know."

"Yeah," said Ruth. "It made me think the same thing."

"It made me proud." Jimmy jutted his chin out. "To think about how strong our people are to have made it through—you know, whippings, hangings, and all that."

"Yeah," said Isaac. "If we can overcome that"—first he gestured to Jimmy and Taylor, but then his little peanut arms gestured to all of us—"we can overcome anything."

I knew what they were all trying to do. To rally my spirits. And I appreciated it and all, but the people I came from—they weren't the strong ones. They were the weak ones.

Mr. Phelps had been hanging back, listening, but now he spoke. "The past can't be undone, Maebelle. The only thing we can do is learn from it. That's what historians do."

I stared at my lap, not wanting to look anyone in the eye, but Isaac leaned over and grabbed my hand. He squeezed it, and the surge he sent through me made me raise my head.

"To get to what really happened in the past—to fit all the pieces together—we have to listen to what each part of the puzzle tells us," said Mr. Phelps. "Looks to me like you assembled a bunch of fine historians, Maebelle. You should put them to good use."

"I did?"

Mr. Phelps nodded. "You did. And even if there were no abolitionists at Oak Alley, I surely believe there were some in town, and we're going to find them. So who's ready to do some more digging?"

"I am," said Issac.

"I am," said Ruth.

"Me too," said Taylor.

"What do you think we're doing here?" said Jimmy.

"All right, then," Mr. Phelps said. "Huddle up. I've got plenty enough research to go around."

· 43 ·

Little-Known Fact:
In North Carolina, it is against
the law to plow a cotton field
with an elephant.

If elephants were protected—why
weren't people?

The Secret Society of Historians took to meeting in the early morning out near the blackberry bushes; we were too busy come the afternoons, rehearsing our Clandestine Clogger routine. By the end of the week we each had read or skimmed *Hidden in Plain View* and helped scan at least a thousand of Mr. Phelps's handwritten notes and historical papers. Ruby Red could have been anyone—even Bozo the Clown.

In my fact notebook I jotted down the things we as a group had discovered:

• 25% of all Southern whites owned slaves. Most had no more than three or four. (Jimmy)

• Oak Alley had way more than that. That old Josiah had 25 names listed in his ledger. (Maebelle)

• Mr. Phelps's notes said sometimes white slave owners freed their slaves when they died. They wrote it into their wills. (Isaac)

• In Virginia in the 1850s, a guy named Moncure Conway led 30 of his family's slaves to freedom. The *Washington Post* ran an article about him and showed some pictures of the modern-day descendants of those slaves. (Ruth. Photocopy of article is in here.)

• Ten sources—some of them slave narratives and some of them diaries of plantation owners—mention the abolitionist Ruby Red, a code name for someone who was helping local slaves escape. There was even one flyer advertising a $1,000 reward for his capture. (Taylor)

• Rewards were offered for runaway slaves—some as low as $50 and some as high as $500. (Jimmy)

• It was hard to tell if someone was born free, since there were hardly any birth certificates back then. Free men and women had to carry free papers. They were easy to forge, so almost every black person was suspected of being a slave. (Isaac)

• Quilts weren't just about stories or symbols communicating ways to freedom. Sometimes maps of towns or plantations were sewn into them. (Maebelle. Read that in *Hidden in Plain View*.)

• Mulattos were were half white and half black. Quadroons were 1/8 black. (Isaac. Read that in *The Underground Railroad*, Volume 1.)

• Most escapees left at night and walked, swam, or floated in riverways so dogs sent to chase them couldn't hunt them down. (Jimmy and Ruth)

After a week of digging, that was all we had. We weren't much help to Mr. Phelps at all. Compiling and organizing information that he already had might have been what he intended for us to do, but I had other plans. I wanted—needed—to make a discovery, something to either prove or disprove that anyone at Oak Alley way back when could have been working on the side of freedom. If it hadn't been Josiah T., maybe it had been someone else. The guest ledger mentioned Philip and Melinda Eberlee. Maybe one of them had been Ruby Red.

So one night, while Isaac was sleeping at the Hillibrands' and Ruth was spending the night, she and I snuck back into the locked wing. In the morning I had something new to share.

"Check this out." I gingerly dug some letters from my backpack. I had taken them from Josiah's room and placed each one in a quart-sized ziplock bag, since the paper was thin and could easily crumble. "I think I know what the falling-out was between Charles Turner and Josiah T."

Everyone had settled into their normal seats. Jimmy and Ruth sat on a tree trunk and Isaac and Taylor plopped down on a huge round rock. We'd decided earlier that week that it must've been a marker showing the entrance to where Oak Alley's stone warehouses had once stood. Taylor had pointed out to me that they might not have been warehouses but slave cabins, and that the old dilapidated chimney on top of the hill could've been where the overseer's house was.

"Well, are you going to tell us or what?" asked Jimmy.

"Keep your pants on," said Ruth. "It's worth waiting for."

"A bunch of slaves disappeared from Turner House in the weeks and months leading up to the fire there. They were all related to Hannah V., the slave of Josiah's who wrote down the cobbler recipe," I said.

"They were her family?" Isaac asked.

"Yep, one was her aunt, a slave named Ann. One was her grandfather, a man named Cornelius. And a mean letter Charles Turner's wife wrote mentions a 'mulatto child grown to five or six' who Hannah V. had years earlier. It's dated August 2, 1859. Listen to this . . .

"A father in good stead with his Maker is bound by God to seek shelter and do all manner of good and justly actions to see his son to safety. However, our Good Lord does not deem miscreant offspring between a slave and her owner to be rightly bequeathed the title of son and right hand. Your parents sold Damascus to us. He is our property and he shall stay our property."

I stopped reading. It took me a while to make it through all those big words, and even longer to get the meaning behind them.

Isaac grabbed the letter from me. It would've ripped in half if it hadn't been in plastic. "Are you saying Josiah T. had a baby? A slave baby?"

"You got that out of it? None of it made a lick of sense to me," said Jimmy. "Is that letter written in Shakespeare's English or what?"

"It doesn't say it outright, but it sure sounds like Josiah was trying to get Hannah's child Damascus back. All the other slaves who escaped were related to her. Maybe she was Ruby Red," I said.

"Did Josiah or Hannah have red hair?" Taylor asked.

I shrugged. "I still haven't seen what Josiah looked like. No paintings, no photographs—and even if I did see a photo, it would be in black-and-white. I don't think I could tell what color his hair was. Hannah V.'s either."

"Maybe Ruby Red isn't a clue about hair color. What else could it be code for?" Jimmy asked. He paced back and forth. I had never seen him so serious, not doing tricks on his bike, in clogging rehearsals, or playing Crash 'Em and Dash 'Em.

Ruth plucked at a weed flower that grew near her feet. "I still can't believe people were tallied and treated worse than bushels of hay."

"Or that a baby could be thought of as property, or even worse—what was it that letter said?—a 'miscreant offspring.'" Isaac winced. "What does that even mean?"

I swallowed. I'd looked it up in the dictionary that morning. I'd reckoned it was bad, but what Charles Turner's wife wrote turned out to be ickier than I thought. *Miscreant* meant "depraved or villainous." That was what slavery was, a miscreant institution.

"Who knows. Something stupid, I'm sure," I said, not revealing what I knew. "The important thing is, maybe Josiah T. wasn't as T.-for-Terrible as we thought."

· 44 ·

Little-Known Fact:
A passionate kiss can burn up
6.4 calories.

How many calories does a smooch
burn?

Even after two weeks of rehearsal, the Clandestine
Cloggers could have been renamed the Clumsy Cloggers. Lucinda was not pleased with our efforts. I did my
best to rally the troops, and honestly, they all were trying,
but instead of getting better and better our dancing was
getting worse and worse. Trying to stitch together the
pieces and patches of research and fact-collecting we'd all
been doing for Mr. Phelps had our feet as leaden and
heavy as our hearts.

Today was our last rehearsal, our *v-e-r-y*, very last one.

Isaac and Ruth missed a ball change. Jimmy slipped
when he was gearing up to do a backflip. Taylor seemed to
be the only one able to keep his fast feet moving. Football

tryouts were coming up, and he was taking his training—our clogging—as seriously as our fact-collecting.

The third time I messed up the clog over vine, Lucinda called it a day. "That's it! That's it! Go on and get out of here. No one looks like they're having any fun!"

"We're having fun," I said, sliding off my clogging shoe and rubbing a blister. "Aren't we?"

"Sure." "Totally." "Yep," came the replies.

"Do not lie to me." Lucinda pointed one of her rhinestone-y nails at us. "It is A-OK to be having an off day, especially before a big performance, but y'all have been losing steam for a while now. Is it my teaching?"

"Oh, no," said Isaac. "You and Mrs. Hillibrand have been the best clogging teacher and at-home coach around."

"We've just got other stuff on our minds," said Jimmy.

"Something more important than a blue ribbon?" Lucinda asked, plopping down in a chair.

"Kind of," I said, and then I shook my head. "Not really. The dance contest is important, and we all still want a blue ribbon, but working together"—I eyed the group, hoping they knew what I was getting at: that none of us could have done alone what we'd been doing together—"is what really counts."

Ruth elbowed me. "Listen to you! Once upon a time you were blue-ribbon bound like nothing else mattered."

I smiled, looking over at Isaac and the rest of the worn-out Clandestine Cloggers.

"Lots of stuff matters," I said. I wanted to make Lucinda proud. Granny and Gramps, too. They would be recording the performance on their digital camera to send to Mama and Daddy. They had left Chicago, hit Omaha and Salt Lake City, and now were in San Francisco before going on to Los Angeles.

"Well, the best way to win a blue ribbon tomorrow is to have fun. Let the music move you. Dancing is a celebration. You know, there is an African wedding tradition called jumping the broom," Lucinda said, getting up and beginning to set the dance hall up for when it opened for dinner. "That jump was a celebration, joy over starting a new life. Heck, it could even have influenced clogging. It ain't just mountain folk and the Scotch and the Irish who did step dances."

My eyebrows shot up. The rest of the dance crew was listening intently too. Maybe our dancing wasn't a dismissal of all the slave stuff we had been learning. Maybe our dance could be like those songs Gramps had made up on the spot—one for Isaac and one for me. Maybe it could be an ode to the past.

"Jeepers, y'all skedaddle now. I've got work to do." Lucinda tossed me my spiral notebook—I still tugged it and my lucky purple pen around with me, though the facts I was learning didn't just come from reading books anymore. Lately, they came from living life. "And have some fun. That's an order."

We grabbed our duffel bags, filled our water bottles at the drinking fountain, and left the dark dance hall, walking out into the blinding sunlight.

We hadn't gone too far before Ruth convinced us that Lucinda was right. "It's not like we don't care what happened with Josiah T. and Hannah V. if we have a little fun," she insisted.

"We could even start today," said Jimmy. "Not tomorrow."

"Yeah, it's hot," said Taylor. He pulled the bill of his Atlanta Braves ball cap down. "So—are we going to hit our pool or the swimming hole?" he asked.

"The swimming hole," we chimed.

"And last one there is a rotten egg!" yelled Isaac. He pumped his legs, running toward the Kiss-Me-Quick Bridge, and we all ran after him, not a one of us caring that we didn't have bathing suits in our bags. When we got to the edge of the water, we dove in, clothes and all.

. . .

We played Marco Polo until our throats were sore from screaming. It was a good thing Granny was the singer and not any of us. After a while Isaac and Taylor got out of the water and sat under the shade tree. They were working on tying together the boys' wet drippy shirts, along with the sweaty but not drenched ones they'd worn at our clogging rehearsal, and were creating a shirt-rope so we could play tug-of-war. I eyed them as I floated on the water.

On the outside, it sure did look like we had had a fun day. And we had. But on the inside, my gut was all eaten up with what we had read in that latest historical find.

We hadn't shown it to Mr. Phelps yet, and I wasn't sure we would get to, what with the Anniversary Spectacular tomorrow. I thought about Josiah T.'s tankard, lent by Granny to be on exhibition under glass at the Town of Tweedle Memorabilia Tent. Did that letter Charles Turner's wife wrote really hint at what had happened: that the old friends had become enemies because of something to do with the fugitive slaves related to Hannah V.—and her son?

I stared at the clouds. It wasn't fair: even after all this digging, the questions kept coming. It was worse than solving a puzzle or a riddle. Even if we spent this summer and next and all the summers after that right here in Tweedle, I was beginning to think we'd never have an answer. An honest and true one. One I could memorize and stick in my fact notebook with all the others.

Ugh! All those questions that swam around inside me—about Josiah, Hannah V., Charles Turner, and Ruby Red—were doing nothing more than giving me a headache. I flipped underwater and swam toward the shore.

"I'll play the winner of the first round," I said to Isaac and Taylor as I attempted to yank myself out of the murky water. My T-shirt and denim shorts were so wet and weighed down, it made pushing my booty onto the grassy knoll even harder than usual. I turned so my butt would hit the edge first. Then I plunked my palms facedown, and as I was hoisting myself up, I saw the strangest thing!

Cast out onto the water under the bridge were two

shadows. One leaned in to kiss the other. Just like the bridge's name said, the kiss was quick. I blinked, thinking I was somehow seeing the ghost of Josiah kissing one of the local ladies or Hannah V. or whoever, but there was no mistaking who the two figures were: Ruth and Jimmy!

Little-Known Fact:
No one knows where the famous
composer Mozart is buried.

The same could be said for
Josiah T.

"So is everybody ready for the big day tomorrow?"
asked Gramps.

There was no Eberlee Explosion rehearsal tonight.
Though practice could make you perfect, Gramps was a
firm believer in enough being enough.

After supper, we'd strolled downtown and gotten ice
cream cones at the five-and-dime and watched the crews
work on hanging the last of the banners and other decora-
tions at the bandstand. A makeshift stage had been at-
tached to it, and that was where the clogging competition
would be held. All over Tweedle Park there would be
stations set up for judging the Tastiest Tomato and the
Best Fried Fritter and the Most Delicious Dessert—not to

mention the Memorabilia Tent, where Granny would be showing off the tankard.

"Yep, more than ready," said Isaac. "I finished my song. Now I've just got to give it a name."

"I'm sure you'll think of something," I said as I turned a cartwheel on the grass.

Gramps and Isaac set up camp on the front porch. They got out the checkerboard and got to double-jumping and kinging one another. Granny flipped through a magazine. She wasn't reading one on needlepoint or other grandmotherly pursuits—she was reading the latest *Rolling Stone* as she rocked in her rocker.

"You can take the musician out of the biz, but you can't take the biz out of the musician," she'd said when she nabbed a copy downtown.

Me? I couldn't stop thinking about Ruth and Jimmy down at the Kiss-Me-Quick. Maybe, if only for a moment, the spirit of Josiah T. had been trying to tell me something.

I flipped hand-hand-foot-foot, hand-hand-foot-foot, doing cartwheel after cartwheel, trying to figure out what it was.

I hadn't been the only witness to the clandestine (a word Jimmy had readily worked into his vocabulary) kiss. Taylor had seen them a second or two after I had, and he had started clapping, giving his brother a standing ovation. "Whoo-hoo, little brother landed one at the Kiss-Me-Quick!" He was so excited that Isaac high-fived him, but I don't think Isaac knew what for.

I yanked Ruth to the side of the road on the way home.

"What was all that about?" I'd asked.

"Oh, all the boys going into sixth grade have a bet to see if they can kiss a girl at the Kiss-Me-Quick before the summer is up," Ruth explained.

"You let Jimmy Hillibrand kiss you for a bet?"

"It's not like he asked me," Ruth said. "It was over before I knew it."

"Closed mouth?" I asked.

"Yep," said Ruth.

"Good!"

We all made smoochy and kissy noises as we walked home from the swimming hole. When the turnoff came for Ruth's dad's house, she waved goodbye, paying no more attention to Jimmy than she did to the rest of us.

I felt a tug in my chest as I realized that Ruth had gotten what she wanted out of the summer—to kiss a boy—and Isaac had gotten what he wanted too—to not be the one and only. I was glad they had gotten what they wanted, even if what I wanted—to get back into G & T—was never going to happen. That desire had been replaced. I'd had the great good fortune to stumble on a mystery, and solving it was going to be better than acing a silly placement test.

I turned more cartwheels as the sun continued to sink in the sky. As I went from right side up to upside down and back, the colors of the sky—pinks, oranges, reds—blurred together. It was like a mix of all sorts of lipstick colors.

I giggled to myself. All that talk of kissing must've

gotten to me. Why else would I compare the sunset to lipstick?

Maybe I missed Mama. She let me play with her lipsticks when they got down to little nubs at the end. Back home on my dresser I had Tawny Orange, Pretty in Pink, and the rest of the Ruby Red I'd used for my science experiment. *Ruby Red . . .*

Holy cannoli! Ruby Red!

Jimmy was right! What if the Ruby Red code name didn't refer to hair color? It could be a reference to lips— the kissing instruments. And no one was more known around these parts for kissing than Josiah T.

Sure, it was far-fetched, but codes were tricky. Disguises, too. Harriet Tubman and others had been known to dress in costume to avoid being caught. Had Josiah himself dressed up, or had he disguised the slaves? And did the Kiss-Me-Quick Bridge have anything to do with the escape plans?

A breeze blew and I got goose bumps. I was getting c-l-o-s-e, close to figuring everything out. I could feel it.

· 46 ·

Little-Known Fact:
The heart doesn't stop when you
sneeze.

But mine stops whenever I go into
the locked wing.

I dragged Isaac out of bed. He rubbed his knuckles into his eye sockets and finally plunked his feet onto the floor. He grabbed the flashlight from where he kept it on his nightstand. In the dark, I led him by the hand down both sets of stairs until we reached the locked-wing door. He flicked on the flashlight and shined it at the lock. I'd taken that silver toothpick out of my underwear drawer, where I'd stashed it for safekeeping, and now I turned it in the lock. It took only a minute and then I heard the click.

"I can't believe we didn't think of it before. Josiah T. took a bunch of different ladies to the Kiss-Me-Quick. The bridge is over the water. Slaves often used waterways on their escape routes. The slaves who we know escaped were helped by someone nicknamed Ruby Red. I really, truly think that person was Josiah. I just know we are *this* close to figuring it all out: the fire, the connection to the Railroad, everything. We've just got to look one more time."

"Okay," said Isaac. "But I'm scared, so hold my hand."

I took Isaac's hand and together we stepped into the locked wing.

"Cover your nose," I told him. "It's really dusty in here. I coughed a bunch and I don't have bad allergies."

"I'm only allergic to dogs," Isaac said, but he copied me. When I lifted my pajama top up to cover my nose—nothing showed but my belly button—Isaac did the same. "So what do we need to look for?"

"Not sure. Maybe some old-timey pictures—like the kind in textbooks. Or some more letters or another journal or something. Just keep thinking, what would we need to tie Josiah T. to helping slaves escape?"

We checked the first two rooms together. I held Isaac's hand and he held the flashlight. He shined it wherever I asked him to—in closets, behind bookshelves, over the silver swords and muskets hanging on the walls in the gun room. We worked quietly; the only sounds were the shuffling of our feet and the *boom-bang*ing of our hearts in our chests. To me, my heartbeat was as loud as Winnie backfiring. I was surprised it didn't wake the whole house.

We shut the door to the gun room and crept back into the long hallway. We were about to hit the next room when Isaac tugged on my wrist.

"Since you're the smartest person I know, I want your opinion on something."

"Sure," I whispered.

"Do you think it's true that children of mixed heritage are 'miscreant offspring'?" Isaac asked.

"Way back when, people thought that, but they were wrong and they were stupid. No one thinks that anymore."

"Yes, they do." Isaac's voice was so thin it sounded as threadbare as an old sheet.

I leaned against the wall. "Did someone say something mean to you? Who? We'll tell Gramps and Granny—they won't stand for any kind of bad talk. C'mon, tell me."

Isaac stood close to me. "You're not the only one whose family had backward ideas, but at least yours had them during the Civil War, not after. *Way* after. Like ten years ago."

I had no idea what Isaac was talking about, but he kept on, the words pouring out of him. "Even if Josiah T. wasn't Ruby Red like we hope he is, he's still better than the people whose blood I've got running through me."

"What are you talking about? Your mother was the finest person around, and she fought as long and hard as she could to stay alive—not just for her but for you."

"She told me just before she died . . ."

Isaac swallowed hard and a mess of tears slid down his face. He didn't have any tissue, so I shook out a dusty sheet and gave him the corner to blow his nose.

"After my parents married and had me, my grandparents paid my dad to have nothing to do with me. That's why he left us."

"Why would your mom's parents do that?" I asked, though it explained why Aunt Alice had adopted Isaac and he hadn't gone to live with any grandparents or aunts and uncles.

"No, not them. I never knew them, but Mom told me that if they had lived long enough, they would have wanted to know me. I'm talking about my dad's parents. My white dad's parents."

His white dad.

Now I knew what Isaac was getting at. Why the words in that letter—*miscreant offspring*—were so awful, even more awful than they had first sounded. Someone had thought that about Isaac!

"You listen to me and you listen to me good." I draped a long arm around Isaac and held him close. "Sometimes getting to hear the ugly truth leads to something good. Your dad was dumb, not having the guts to stand up to his parents, but if he had been a stand-up guy you wouldn't be here now. I wouldn't know you. You wouldn't know Aunt Alice, Granny and Gramps, Ruth, Jimmy and Taylor, Mr. Phelps, Lucinda"—I gulped—"or me. And except for me and my bouts of bad behavior, all those folks have been pretty welcoming, haven't they? No one has been mean or called you nasty names?"

"Not unless you count Trumpet Boy or Li'l Bit," Isaac said.

"Well, Trumpet Boy is a compliment, and Granny giving you a nickname is a sign of affection, she's not making fun of you."

"Oh, I know, I kind of like Li'l Bit," Isaac said. "I don't mind being short. You know, when you warm up on the trumpet, you start low but you end with the high notes. That's how I think of me and you. Like opposite ends of a musical scale."

I punched his arm. "Cool. Like you can't have one without the other."

"Exactly," he said, punching me back.

"Ouch." I laughed. For a peanut head he could pack a punch. "Too bad you don't know your birth grandparents' names. If you did, I'd write them a thank-you letter."

"You would?"

"I would—and it would go like this:

"Dear Dingbos,

"Thank you and your son for being the dumbest people on the planet. Because you could not see past the color of your grandson's skin, my family is now *p-e-r-f-e-c-t*, perfect—as in totally complete. That's what Gramps would say, and did! He sang it in a song. That's how much he loves Li'l Bit. How much we all do. So don't you ever think of taking Isaac back. Gramps and Granny could take you in an arm-wrestling contest any day—and if they couldn't, I could! So you just better leave Isaac where he belongs. With us!

"Sincerely but oh-so-not-respectfully yours,
"Maebelle T. (for Tried-and-True) Earl"

Little-Known Fact:
Flowers are used in perfumes
because they produce fragrant
oils.

Did Hannah V. get to wear
perfume?

After our long heart-to-heart, Isaac and I needed to make up time.

"We better split up," I said. "We shouldn't stay down here too long. What if Granny or Gramps wakes up and checks on us?"

I pointed to the room behind me. We didn't have another flashlight, but the moon was bright, and I thought I'd have enough light to make a sweep of the room if I opened the heavy curtains. "You take that room. And if you need me, I'll come running."

"Okay," Isaac said, and he set off with the flashlight, the beam shaking a bit. It was the middle of the night, the time when slaves ran away and barking dogs were set loose after them.

I searched everywhere: inside every book, in every nightstand drawer, under every mattress. I checked the closets and looked in every suit pocket I came across. I found a few photographs stuck in an old desk drawer, and I brought them over to the window to see more clearly. Most were of a bunch of horses grazing in the field, but one was of a pretty woman in front of a row of slave cabins with an infant in her arms. Was that Hannah V.? And Damascus, the baby Josiah might have been trying to save? I closed the study door and went to go find Isaac.

I found him in Josiah T.'s room.

Isaac wasn't searching. He was curled atop the bumpy starry quilt, sound asleep. I fingered the fabric again. This quilt design wasn't mentioned in the book, but I still felt something tug at me whenever I looked at it. The stars were all different sizes, and some of them popped out from the backing like hills.

Was this quilt another piece of the puzzle? I remembered taking notes on how some slave quilts could be maps of mountains ranges, towns, or even something as small—if you could call two hundred to five hundred acres small—as a plantation!

Isaac's flashlight was still on, but it had fallen to the floor. I picked it up and shined it on the bedspread. The largest star could be Oak Alley. There was a red star that was puffy and big, maybe signifying a hill. Maybe it was even marking the overseer's house, because below it were a bunch of squares, plain and drab, not a star among them.

I could have been reading too much into the quilt—I could have—but I didn't think so. I leaned over to shake Isaac awake and ask him what he thought.

Turned out he had found something too. . . . In his arms he held a rag doll. Had it been Josiah's? His son's? He'd had a son with Hannah V. I was sure of it.

Isaac drew in a deep breath. Slowly, he let it out. I didn't have the heart to wake him. He looked so peaceful there on Josiah T.'s bed.

"Keep sleeping, cuz," I whispered to him. "We are *so* on to something."

. . .

A hand shook my shoulder. I had fallen asleep in the bottom of Josiah T.'s closet, where I'd found a trunk of dresses, various sizes from child-sized to big and burly, along with a bunch of bonnets. I was sure they had to be the disguises Josiah T. had dressed the runaway slaves in. What else would he have been doing with a trunkful of women's clothes? I wondered how he got them. Did like-minded folks donate them or did he steal them off laundry lines? I plopped a bonnet on my head and closed my heavy lids for just a second, but after all my searching and scanning my tired eyes had a mind of their own. One long eyelid flutter must've been all it took.

"Just a second, Isaac, I've got dust in my eyes." I picked it out as best I could with my fingernail, but when I opened my eyes, it wasn't Isaac staring at me. It was Gramps.

"What do you think you are doing, Maebelle T.?" He towered over me, wearing his plaid pajamas.

"Gramps, I'm sorry. I know you didn't want us in here. It's just . . . we had to. And you'll never guess what I discovered. It's just a theory, but . . ." I hopped up, but my slipper-covered feet caught on the dress I'd been using as a blanket. I pitched forward and almost took Gramps down with me. He looked mad as all get-out, but he helped me up.

More footsteps ran down the long hall. "You found them! Thank heavens you found them." Granny grabbed us—with all the commotion, Isaac had woken too. Even Cotton came lumbering in.

"I can explain what we're doing in here," I said. "And it has nothing to do with Isaac; I made him come with me."

"To the kitchen, now," Gramps said, taking me by my shoulder and marching me down the hall.

Isaac followed, clutching the dusty rag doll he had found. "Look! Do you think this was that Damascus kid's—the kid from the letter?" he asked me.

I nodded. I didn't know anything for sure, but I hoped so.

· · ·

Once we got to the kitchen, Gramps pointed for me to sit down. Isaac, too.

"Ivory Ann, would you feed these two ragamuffins some breakfast? I'm going to take Winnie for a spin and clear my head."

Granny patted Gramps's hand. "Don't be too long. We're supposed to be headed to the spectacular soon. And don't be so hard on Butter Bean. I was curious too." She held her thumb and pointer finger about an inch apart. "I was this close to calling a locksmith to get me on in there—but I reckon these grandkids of ours beat me to it."

Gramps's face fell. Granny's admission seemed to do him in. I remembered what Granny had said about how some families built fences topped with barbed wire and some threw the windows open. I reckoned she was trying to tell Gramps that we'd always been a windows-open kind of family and we shouldn't let anything change that. Not this house. Not the locked wing. Not the past.

Gramps stroked his beard, then kissed Granny goodbye. "Y'all go ahead and walk to the town square. I've got an errand to do. I'll meet you there." He turned to me. "As soon as our performances are all over, we are going to have a mighty long talk, Maebelle. You got me?"

"Yes, sir," I said.

"It wasn't Maebelle's fault. She didn't twist my arm," Isaac said. "And I was wrong when I told you not to read that letter from Edith. It's better to know stuff than to stay in the dark."

"You may be right about that, but the two of you broke the rules, and for that we have to have a talk." Gramps headed upstairs to get dressed. He came down as I was telling Granny all about everything we'd found, and everything Isaac, the Hillibrand boys, and Ruth and I had written in my notebook. "Bring my costume with you, Ivory Ann," he yelled, and then he stepped out the front door, taking Cotton with him—and not stopping in to say goodbye.

· 48 ·

Little-Known Fact:
The first person to be caught under the Fugitive Slave Act of 1850 was James Hamlet. He would have been sent back to slavery had the people of Syracuse not raised enough money to be sure that didn't happen. They had to "buy" his freedom.

I hate it that back then, freedom had to be bought. Did Ruby Red hate it too?

Throngs of people milled through the town square. The Hillibrands walked with us, and Jimmy and Taylor kept stopping to talk to kids they knew from school, introducing Isaac and me as their next-door neighbors. We met up with Ruth and her dad as we entered Tweedle Park, and he left her with us while he went off to scope out some good seats for the dance competition. He planned on saving some for him, the Hillibrands, and Gramps and Granny so our cheering section would all be in one place.

Jimmy flung his arm around Ruth's shoulders. "After we earn our blue ribbon, what do you say we take a stroll to the Kiss-Me-Quick?"

"Why wait?" Ruth made a fish face. "Pucker up," she said, making smoochy noises.

"Ewww, I hope your face doesn't freeze that way," Jimmy said.

Ruth swatted him on the shoulder. Jimmy pushed her back, and then Ruth was off and chasing him, and Isaac was trailing after the both of them. My eyes followed them running through the crowd; I was hoping I'd catch sight of Gramps.

We rounded the corner onto Main. All the mom-and-pop shops had their doors propped wide open, and orange cones closed off the road to traffic. There was face painting and balloon tying, and there were long picnic tables in the center of the road where everyone could eat after the judges announced the blue ribbons for Best Burger, Best Fried Fritter, Tastiest Chili—and of course, Most Delicious Dessert. Yep, there was no way I would have won that unless Cotton was the judge.

Out in the grassy field there were potato-sack races, kids rolling hard-boiled eggs with spoons, and even a frog-jumping contest. All in the honor of the town's 175th anniversary.

"How're you feeling, Butter Bean?" Granny asked. "Any jitters?"

"Just a few," I said. "I'll feel better when Gramps makes it. He was awfully mad this morning. I'd never seen him so angry."

Granny tweaked my nose. "After forty-five-or-so-odd years of marriage, I know my husband. Angus T. will come around, just you wait and see. Now, where did Issac run off to?" Granny asked, spinning in a circle amid the mass of people and the growing festivities. "It's almost time for y'all to go on."

"There he is, with Ruth and the Hillibrand boys," I said, seeing Ruth in her swirly skirt. "Oh, look, they've already changed."

Granny handed me my outfit. "There's a ladies' room back thataway. Let's go get you dolled up."

. . .

We neared the edge of the stage. An all-girl jazz group, Razzmatazz, was up there now. I stood on my tiptoes to see if they were any good, and to see where the judge sat. Then I saw her, all right: Miss Trina Von Decker. Her silver hair was spritzed and sprayed to within an inch of her life.

The girls up there were good. They were all about Taylor's age; I could tell they were wearing bras and had makeup on. I hadn't thought of asking Granny about wearing any lipstick or blush, let alone glitter on my face, neck, and shoulders like the girls in Razzmatazz. I tugged at the ruffles on my blouse—Granny had made one for me and one for Ruth. Watching those girls, I felt silly in my dance outfit, which was a red swirly skirt topped with the frilly white blouse. Jimmy, Taylor, and Isaac, those lucky ducks, were wearing stretchy dance blue jeans with plain white T-shirts, but they had to wear sport coats over them so they'd look like mini-businessmen in the nine-to-five workaday world.

"Hey, y'all, over here. It's getting close to showtime." Lucinda waved us all over to where she stood near the stairs to the stage. "Y'all look spiffy. Now, who here is ready to have some fun?"

"We are!" the five of us yelled. We formed a circle, put our hands into the center, and then shouted, "THE CLANDESTINE CLOGGERS!" in one unified voice. I never had been part of a team before—I'd been too busy studying for my G & T classes. My butterflies settled down when I reminded myself I wasn't going out there alone.

"Good, that's the spirit. You guys are going to do great. Just remember to keep time in your head, and if any steps get messed up just keep on going," Lucinda said.

"Hello there!" a voice called.

Miss Martha, Lucinda's sister, sauntered over, pushing Stoney in a stroller. I had told Isaac the truth about the diaper, but I'd never paid for my dumb deed, and I deserved to.

"Look at these cute cloggers," Miss Martha said as she hugged her sister hello, and then to Ruth and me, she added: "Remember me?"

"Course we do," I said, for the both of us, and before I

could change my mind I rattled off what I hoped would be a fair punishment. "I just want to let you know, I'm free to babysit any Friday night for as long as I am in Tweedle."

"Bless your heart," Miss Martha said. "How much do you charge?"

"Nothing," I said.

"Well, if today isn't my lucky day, then I don't know what is." Miss Martha clapped her hands as if she had won the lottery. "Uh-oh, looks like it's time. We better take our seats."

Granny gave Isaac and me a quick hug. "Now, you break a leg," she said. "And know your gramps and I are right proud of you two." She rushed off to where Ruth's dad and Mr. and Mrs. Hillibrand were saving two seats, one for her and one for Gramps. His was empty.

I eyed Isaac, and we both seemed to be thinking the same thing: *If Gramps is so proud of us, then why isn't he here?*

· 49 ·

Little-Known Fact:
To escape slavery, one man,
Henry "Box" Brown, mailed
himself from Richmond to
Philadelphia.

Can you believe that?

We hightailed it up the stairs to the main stage, and as Lucinda went to cue up our music, I searched the crowd for Gramps. He should have been easy to see from up there, but I didn't see him at all.

It was time to face a cold hard fact: Gramps was so mad that he didn't want to see us dance.

I thought I might cry, but the fiddle started. Ruth and I were to enter the stage from the right, while the boys would enter from the left. I hoped no one could hear my knocking knees. I was downright scared.

My palms and underarms were sweating but good, and it had nothing to do with the heat and everything to do with all the people standing around watching and waiting.

"You'll be great," Ruth said. "And we'll win that blue ribbon."

"How do you know?" I asked.

"I'm psychic," Ruth said.

I chuckled. Ruth could make me laugh even when I was at my lowest low. Before I knew it, Dolly Parton's voice boomed from the loudspeakers, and we clogged it out onto the stage.

Left. Left. Right. Right. Left. Left. Right. Right. Right. Right. Left. Left. Right. Left. We went from the clog over vine straight into the karate kick, back to the double basic pause, and into the Charleston. We hoofed and huffed all around. Granny clapped, and I could see her out there singing along with Miss Dolly Parton. I closed my eyes for a half second, letting the music move me. I pop-pop-popped, keeping my back straight and my legs flying as if I was a popcorn kernel over a hot flame.

The wind whipped as we shuffled from one side of the stage to the other. Jimmy cut and Taylor moved around me, and then we lined up diagonally and did another clog over vine. It was getting near the end of the song, and it was almost time for the big lift. Isaac got into position; he stopped high-stepping long enough to pull Ruth under his legs and then hoist her in the air.

I kept my feet moving—counting out the lefts and rights in my head, but everything started moving in slow motion as Isaac actually did pull her under. When she came up, she was facing him, and from where I was a few feet behind him I saw her face. As she got tugged up into the air, she mouthed to him: *It's you I like, not Jimmy.*

I was going into my own three-quarter spin, moving into position between Taylor and Jimmy, when I heard the thud.

As I'd been spinning around, Ruth had hit the ground. I reckoned Isaac was in such a state of shock that he must have lost his grip and somehow dropped her.

The music kept going, but the audience stopped clapping. Everyone must have been wondering if Ruth was all right.

Keep going. I kept clogging, and danced over to where Isaac stood frozen like a deer in headlights. I got as close to him as I could—I had broken formation, but Jimmy and Taylor were trying to distract the audience as best they could by doing windmills. "Ruth, are you okay? Can you dance?"

She nodded, beaming up at Isaac.

"You hear that, Isaac, she's okay. Now get dancing."

Isaac held his hand out and Ruth took it. Their feet didn't get to moving right away. "I'm sorry," Isaac said, and right then and there in front of all of Tweedle he leaned in and kissed Ruth on the cheek.

The audience roared. Some folks muttered "Awww" and some folks clapped. With everyone back on their feet together as a team, we moved into the slur and brush step and then right into the double with a rock step.

I was both happy and sad—the same feeling as when I had listened to Isaac playing his trumpet on the back porch—when the last notes of "9 to 5" faded away.

Surely we hadn't won any blue ribbons. The look on Judge Trina Von Decker's face when Ruth fell had told me that. But I didn't mind one bit. I was sad because I'd hurt Gramps—hurt him so much that he had stayed away.

The audience clapped loudly even though the routine hadn't been perfect. The sound of it made me tingle inside. We lined up, both Isaac and Taylor grabbing my hands and Jimmy and Isaac grabbing Ruth's, and we bowed.

We rose and the clapping continued. "Whoo-hoo! Those are my grandkids," I could hear Granny hoot above the sound of all those hands. But her seat was empty. Ruth, Taylor, and Jimmy descended the stairs, but Isaac and I glanced around. I felt dizzy and confused, like the day I'd showed up in Tweedle and Granny and Gramps weren't there to greet me. Something was going on, but I didn't know what.

"Boo-roo-roo," Cotton barked. Gramps bounded up onto the stage with Granny beside him and Cotton on his leash. He tugged Isaac and me into a big bear hug, but there was no room to spin us around.

"Did you see us dance?" I asked.

"I sure did," he said as his whiskers grazed my cheek. "I wouldn't have missed it for the world."

I could barely see with the tears filling my eyes—or feel my feet, since Cotton had plopped his booty down on them both.

· 50 ·

Little-Known Fact:
The Truth with a capital *T* can't
always be proved.

But for it to be real, it's only got to
be believed.

Gramps tapped the microphone as the crowd settled back down and took their seats. Granny came on-stage, wearing her regular old clothes—a tie-dyed sun-dress that skimmed the floor—and she brought up two stools, one for me and one for Isaac. We sat, along with the rest of Tweedle, wondering what was going on.

Granny didn't seem to have a clue either. She held on to Cotton's leash.

"This here is my wife, Ivory Ann. We promised we would play as the Eberlee Explosion, and play we will, but instead of doing it now while the judges are all deciding on today's blue-ribbon winners, we're going to play in the town square tonight after the sun goes down. A real live outdoor dance hall. Do y'all think Diamond Dave will mind?"

"Nooooooooooooooo," the crowd replied all together. And folks buzzed with the news of a real dance to take place under the stars.

"Glad to see this idea has been met with approval. Mrs. Mayor Eliza Fitzwhelm thought it would be," Gramps said. He gestured to his left, and the rotund Mrs. Mayor came out and took a bow. The townspeople hooted and hollered, and when the applause died down, Gramps helped her down the stairs and off the stage.

"But since we have this time too, we are going to use it. You've met Ivory Ann and my grandkids, Maebelle and Isaac, who tore up the stage in the last number along with the rest of the Clandestine Cloggers," Gramps said as the crowd broke into a smattering of applause. "But what you don't know is that these two kids here have torn a hole in my heart."

I gulped. Was that what Isaac and I had done? Torn a hole in his heart? If so, it was all my fault, not Isaac's. I stood to tell Gramps that, but he continued to address the town.

"How many of you here knew Edith Eberlee?" Gramps asked.

A ton of hands went up.

"And how many of you knew her to be an odd one? Hardly ever leaving her house, and surely never ever letting anyone inside?"

The same number of hands stayed up. Maybe even more.

"What is he doing?" I asked Granny.

"You got me," she said, whispering in my ear and waving out to all the people watching us, trying not to show that she was as nervous as I was about whatever was coming next.

"Well, what you don't know, I didn't want to know either. But these two brave kids here didn't really give me a choice. They face things head-on, even if it means going against an elder's orders. Especially then, because they're good kids. Not outlaws."

Gramps winked at me. Whatever was coming was going to be okay.

"So before arriving here today, I took a cue from them and decided to face some things I haven't wanted to face. I took a ride over to the Tweedle branch bank to get my safe-deposit box, and I got my hands on a letter my aunt Edith left me. One that I was too scared to read until I got a glimpse of Isaac and Maebelle sleeping after sneaking into Oak Alley's locked wing."

An *ooooohhhh* circled around. My ears tingled. Gramps sure was taking down the Eberlee barbed wire and throwing wide the windows. Everyone in town knew about the locked wing, and now they would want to know what was in there.

"Maebelle T., what did you find?" Mr. Phelps broke through the crowd—he didn't push anyone, but folks stepped to the side so he could make it to the lip of the stage. Like always, he had on a seersucker suit.

The entire crowd was quiet. I could feel their anticipation even more than when Isaac had dropped Ruth and everyone had been waiting to see if she would be A-OK.

"I'm pretty sure Josiah was Ruby Red. I think the quilt

on his bed is a map of the plantation. I took some pictures of it—maybe we can compare it to a land deed or something. And I may have found a picture of Hannah V.," I rattled off as fast as I could.

"Huh?" "Ruby Red?" "What is she talking about?" "Who is Hannah V?" the crowed murmured one to another.

"Oh, we will get to that. My granddaughter is an A-one detective," Gramps said.

"I am?" I asked.

"Yep," Gramps said, ruffling my hair. He turned to the crowd. "I read the letter Aunt Edith left me before I left the bank, and I'm going to read it to everyone here, as it affects us all. It's time we all face the truth together."

Gramps cleared his throat, a clue that he was nervous. Granny left Isaac and me and went to him, to add her strength to his. Gramps spoke into a cordless microphone, his voice booming, loud and strong.

" 'I choose to leave you Oak Alley since you and your wife had the gumption to follow your dreams, and gumption is something I always was and am sorely lacking. If I had any, I would change the instructions in my will, ordering you not to leave the wing locked, but to turn it open for all to see.' "

The crowd hung on Gramps's every word—or rather, Aunt Edith's.

" 'You may be asking why it got locked in the first place. When you were just a boy, Angus, and I was a young woman, I discovered a secret that ripped our family apart.

I found a bundle of letters, tied with a ribbon that smelled like blackberries, in the hollow post of a four-poster bed. I read them, I read them all. Love letters is what they were. When I read the last one, I knew it couldn't have ended well. The date the lovers were to meet corresponded to the date of the big fire at Turner House—August 4, 1859. I took the letters to my father and Henry, your father. They were in the parlor. Y'all were visiting from Valdosta that day.

"'My father read the first one to himself, and without consulting anyone, he threw the bundle in the fire. Then and there he ordered me to not breathe a word of what I had read, but I told Henry. I had to. He was my brother.

"'Henry wanted to tell the town. Document what we had learned, write an article on it for the *Tweedle Gazette*. But Father wouldn't hear of it. He kicked your father out of Oak Alley—and told him never to return. Sadly, he never did.

"'From that day on, the west wing was locked. We never talked about what I had discovered. I lived with Mother and Father until they passed, so I couldn't do anything about it, but even after they passed, I am sad to say that I obeyed Father's orders to not speak a word of this to any living soul.'"

Gramps held the letter and the microphone out to me. "Maebelle, will you read the rest?"

I stayed seated. My eyes went to Mr. Phelps. He nodded.

I slid off the stool, my legs shakier than when I was

clogging. I took the letter and the mike and started where Gramps had left off.

"'I found the letters in the 1940s,'" I read, "'and things were so different then. Father feared the town would judge us harshly for the family's actions. You see, Josiah T. Eberlee, the youngest son of Philip and Melinda Eberlee, had been in love with a black woman. A slave. One his parents owned. Her name was Hannah V.'"

The crowd gasped. My heart seized up.

"Mr. Phelps, did you hear that? Josiah was in love with Hannah V.!"

"I heard it, all right," said Mr. Phelps. "So did every ear here. Read on, Maebelle. Let the truth be known."

"'Not only did he love this woman, this slave'"—my voice sounded strange to my own ears—"'he wanted to help her escape to freedom—to Canada—along with their child. His parents sold the baby to Charles Turner, which is why I think he and Hannah V. planned to meet there. Josiah T. had already helped to free Hannah's mother, her grandfather, and her aunt and uncle by coming up with an ingenious plan. Whether it was a woman escaping or a man, the slave was given a bonnet and a dress . . .'"

I stopped reading and told the crowd, "That's exactly how I thought Josiah T. did it! I was right! Totally right!" Even my goose bumps had goose bumps!

The crowd broke into applause. I took a cue from Isaac and grinned, soaking it up like a pancake soaks up syrup.

Ruth clapped and laughed. She was standing with her father, who had his hands on her shoulders.

"Finish the letter," said Taylor. He stood huddled with

Jimmy and the rest of his family. Everyone there—everyone in the entire town—hung on every word.

I cleared my throat and flipped the page. I began reading where I had left off. "'It seems Josiah would escort the "lady" down to where a stream from Lake Tweedle emptied, creating a pool of deep water. A bridge had just been built there, and in the hours after dusk had turned to darkness the slave would remove his or her disguise. Under the dress the slave would be wearing regular work clothes or clothes Josiah had provided. Then the escapee would swim off into the lake or paddle a raft that had been hidden along the banks farther up.'"

I looked out at Mr. Phelps. He smiled at me—a sad smile, but one that let me know it was okay to read on. Still, my heart, which was beating overtime, couldn't take any more.

I passed the letter and the mike to Isaac. He was part of our family—maybe not by blood, but in the way that mattered.

"'It was a risky venture,'" he read. "'If caught, Josiah could have been killed, and in the end, he may have been. That fire could have been set to trap Josiah or it could have been set to help him cover his tracks. But I like to believe all three of them got away. Josiah T., Hannah V., and their child. Whether they lived or died trying to find their way to freedom may not matter—what matters most is that they fought to be together.'"

I didn't know if Isaac was thinking about his daddy, a man who didn't have courage enough to stand up to his parents and stay with the woman he loved and their baby, but I was. The letter got passed once more, this time to Granny.

She reached out the hand that held Cotton's leash and took Gramps's hand. She continued on. "'But truthfully, all I know is what I read in those letters—of their deepest love for one another. But I am the only one who ever has known, and I have carried their secret love with me all these years—I have lived on that love, since I never had a love of my own.'" Granny stopped to wipe a tear from her eye.

Aunt Edith's letter came full circle, back to Gramps. He read the last of it, in a voice that was as soft and strong as one of his bear hugs. "'I let Father shame me into thinking this would ruin our family name, but what Josiah did is not something to be ashamed of. I knew if I told you, Angus, you would see to it that it brings the Eberlees honor. Please do so; it is my greatest wish.'"

Everyone out in the audience stood, clapping and clapping—a standing ovation, though there was no hooting or hollering. It was a rousing round of applause but a respectful one too. Aunt Edith's letter said she wanted that locked wing open to everyone. Gramps hadn't said what that meant, but I had an idea. We could put a velvet rope up in the foyer and use the Oak Alley guest ledger as a way to welcome everyone. The entire town could come, one by one, and write their name and why they were there and what they had come to see.

The clapping didn't die down. It went on so long and it was so loud I thought my ears would burst.

"You hear that, Maebelle?" Isaac asked. "All of those people clapping—that's all for you."

"Nope," I said, motioning for Ruth, Mr. Phelps, and the Hillibrand boys to come onstage. Deep down, I knew the real truth. "It's for all of us—but mostly for Hannah V. and Josiah T. and their son."

· 51 ·

Little-Known Fact:
It is said that the painter Paul
Cézanne taught a parrot to say
"Cézanne is a great painter."

If that's true, it's too bad Cézanne
didn't have a family like mine. He
would've known for a fact how
truly *g-r-e-a-t,* great he was.

"*Good evening, town of Tweedle, this here is Jumping Joe—that's right, your fav-o-rite WKIT deejay—and I am broadcasting live right here from beside the Anniversary Spectacular stage. We want to wish all our blue-ribbon winners a big congrats, and we send out a special thank-you to Trina Von Decker for coming in from Hotlanta to judge the dance-dance-dance competition. She is only sorry that she couldn't pick more than one winner. But those are the rules, folks, and pick one she did. Would Razzmatazz stand and please take a bow?*

"Oh, now, ain't they sweet. Congratulations, girls. You had

me so dizzy as you danced I thought I was seeing double. Oh, two of you are twins! Well, then that's why. Ha! All right, everybody settle on down, take your seat, and together let's beat this heat.

"To top off all of today's revelations . . . the promised main attraction is soon to take the stage, so who here is ready for a rootin' tootin' concert? . . . I can't hear you! . . . Oh, now I can. It sounds like all y'all are ready, so without further ado, let's welcome the band!

"On trumpet, Isaac 'Li'l Bit' Johnson! On vocals, Ivory Ann! On guitar, Angus T.! On tambourine, the one and only . . . Miss Maebelle T.!

"For their first ditty, they will be performing an original song by none other than Isaac. It's called 'Thanks for Leaving Me a Family.'

"Let's hear it for the Eberlee Explosion!"

Author's Note

Is there such a thing as the quilt code? Is it fact or is it fiction?

The story of hidden clues sewn into quilts is told in the book Mr. Phelps gives Maebelle. *Hidden in Plain View: A Secret Story of Quilts and the Underground Railroad,* by Jacqueline L. Tobin and Raymond G. Dobard, PhD, is a real book that suggests that some of the symbols and patterns used in slave quilts may have been brought from Africa and were used in planning the escapes of people from bondage. Your local library may have *Hidden in Plan View* on its shelves.

This book is a fine and fascinating read that proved to me that a quilt code could exist. I am no historian; I am not even a budding one, as Maebelle is. What I am is a storyteller, one who fell in love with the stories that have been swirling around slave quilts, which are almost as old as the quilts themselves. These oral stories were passed on from great-grandmother to granddaughter, from great-grandfather to grandson. Oral tradition is a large component of African

American history, and like all oral histories, it can be shaped over and over in the telling, but in the end an essence of truth remains. To me, sewing a quilt and quilting a story serve the same purpose: they each provide warmth and help us connect our past to our present. However, there are historians who question the existence of the quilt code as interpreted by Ozella McDaniel Williams, the primary source mentioned in *Hidden in Plain View*. One of these historians is Giles R. Wright, the director of the New Jersey Historical Commission's Afro-American History program. It is a part of his life's work to be sure that anything associated with the Underground Railroad is well documented and does not rely too heavily on conjecture, as he believes the code in *Hidden in Plain View* does.

So, where does this leave us? As Maebelle examines her family's own slave-owning past, she discovers that "the Truth with a capital *T* can't always be proved. But for it to be real, it's only got to be believed."

That, for me, is enough. It is what keeps me reading about the myths, mysteries, and tried-and-true facts regarding the Underground Railroad—those who helped others escape, those who themselves escaped, and all those who died in the fight for freedom.

Acknowledgments

I owe heartfelt thanks to the many who kept my gumption going in the writing of this book. Norma Fox Mazer cheered me on when Miss Maebelle and Granny were broken down on the side of the road. Tim Wynne-Jones, you too played and sang with Maebelle way back when. Thank you for your song-writing expertise.

To my writing community, the Champagne Sisters: Laurie Calkhoven, Kekla Magoon, and Josanne LaValley and our West Coast member, Connie Kirk, you've each added to these pages and to me as their author. Thank you for our Thursday nights! To the Give Me Fifty folks: Alicia Potter, Sundee T. Frazier, Karmen Koyers, Kerry Leaf, and Lynn Hazen, thanks for our two-hour-long conference calls. To Sarah Aronson, for the first-draft rough read. To Pat Cummings, for being the kindest drill instructor ever. Long live boot camp. To J. E. Macleod and Sarah Sullivan, for reading and responding and urging me on as my deadline drew near.

To all those at FD, especially Ed Reilly, Mark McCall, Cara O'Brien, Gordon McCoun, Pat Keough, Sherrie Weldon, Brian Maddox, Lou Colasuonno, Nic Platt, Sue Bloomberg, and Cathy Davis, thank you for the support. And a special thanks to MJ "Document Saver" McLang for the document retrievals.

To DawnMarie Kerper, for kicking up her cowboy boots and taking me to hear country music in NYC. To Amy Botelho, whose volunteer work at Austin's Helping Hands Home for children is an inspiration. To my sister, Katie Simmons, who has more guts and gumption than anyone I know. To Richard Irving, for being a truth-teller who gives the best bear hugs. To Hollie Hunt, for following her dreams.

To Simi Malone, for allowing me to use a variation of her name, and a reference to her beautiful curls. To Monica Mead and all the kids at Center Stage Dance Academy, where she teaches. Thanks for being my clogging fact-checkers.

To my agent, Regina Brooks, for going above and beyond and for her continued faith in my abilities.

To my editor, Michelle Poploff, and assistant editor Rebecca Short, you are both *extraordinaire,* and that's a fact. Thank you for making me go deeper each go-round and pointing me in the right direction. I'd follow where you both lead anytime, anywhere. To my copy editor, Colleen Fellingham, for her fine eye and fact-checking. If any errors occur, they are mine and mine alone.

To my parents, Allan and Beth Hegedus, for sealing my fate by moving the family to Georgia. To the Bells, the Browns, and the rest of the Hegedus crew, and to all those who've ever been to the Kiss-Me-Quick Bridge: family is family. Our hearts have been healed.

And I would be remiss not to thank deeply and humbly Jacqueline L. Tobin and Raymond G. Dobard, PhD, for their fascinating book, *Hidden in Plain View: A Secret Story of Quilts and the Underground Railroad,* and the late Ozella McDaniel Williams, the keeper of the quilts. Though Ozella didn't live to see the scholarship she inspired in print, it is because of her that kids like Maebelle and Isaac, Northerners and Southerners alike, will always be attracted to the mystery that is the history of the Underground Railroad.

About the Author

Bethany Hegedus has spent time above and below the Mason-Dixon Line. She spent her formative years in Georgia and Illinois and now makes her home in Austin, Texas. Bethany cares deeply for children and is a former high school teacher and youth advocate. She holds an MFA in writing for children and young adults from Vermont College of Fine Arts. This is her second children's book. Please visit her at www.bethanyhegedus.com.